AUTOMATIC EVE

ROKURO INUI

AUTOMATIC EVE

ROKURO INUI

TRANSLATED BY MATT TREYVAUD

HAIKA
SORU

SAN FRANCISCO

Automatic Eve
KIKOU NO EVE
Copyright © Rokuro Inui 2014
English translation rights arranged with SHINCHOSHA Publishing Co., Ltd.
through Japan UNI Agency, Inc., Tokyo

English translation © 2019 VIZ Media, LLC
Cover and interior design by Shawn Carrico

HAIKASORU
Published by VIZ Media, LLC
P.O. Box 77010
San Francisco, CA 94107

www.haikasoru.com

Library of Congress Cataloging-in-Publication Data

Names: Inui, Rokurō, 1971- author. | Treyvaud, Matt, translator.
Title: Automatic Eve / Rokuro Inui ; translated by Matt Treyvaud.
Other titles: Kikō no ibu. English
Description: San Francisco : Haikasoru, [2018]
Identifiers: LCCN 2019006396 | ISBN 9781974708079
Subjects: LCSH: Robots--Fiction. | Empresses--Fiction.
Classification: LCC PL871.5.N88 K5513 2019 | DDC 895.63/6--dc23
LC record available at https://lccn.loc.gov/2019006396

Printed in the U.S.A.

First printing, August 2019

AUTOMATIC EVE

(0)

Beyond the back gate lay a dim, cramped alleyway that ran between the high wooden buildings to Tengen Street.

Both sides of the alley were lined with slatted shelves stacked high with great jars of pickled ginger. They left barely enough room for one man to pass and filled the alley with a sickly vinegar smell.

Nizaemon Egawa came through the gate as though sleep-walking on uncertain legs.

How could this have happened?

Leaning against one of the pickle jars to catch his breath, he looked down at his open hand.

It was red to the elbow with blood.

Blood that was not his own.

He raised the hand to his mouth and licked his palm hesitantly. Metallic, with a hint of salt. Still warm.

This was not like the stories he had heard. There was no stink of oil, no quicksilver gleam. This was human blood, almost black in the dim light.

He lied to me.

Vinegar smarted in his nose with every ragged breath he drew.

Rage boiled within him.

His hand went to the hilt of the two-foot katana he wore in a scabbard at his waist. He popped the guard with his thumb and slid the blade partway out.

Like his hand, it was slick with dark gore. He had neglected to shake the blood off after using it a few moments earlier and had put it away wet. Fortunately, he saw no nicks in the edge.

He decided to go, right now, to the home of the man who had deceived him, force his way in, and cut him down where he stood.

He slid the sword back into its scabbard.

Kyuzo Kugimiya.

As Nizaemon walked toward Tengen Street, the memory of his first meeting with Kyuzo less than a year ago returned to him unbidden...

1

"You're a bird from the south," Nizaemon murmured.

The bird was large and brilliantly colored. It was tethered by a thin chain to a perch made of an unpainted tree branch protruding from a black lacquered box. The box was about four feet high, with mother-of-pearl inlay.

"A macaw, did you call it? I've never seen one before."

The bird's back was lapis lazuli blue, while its breast feathers were yellow as kerria flowers. It opened its black beak as if yawning, then puffed out its chest and spread its wings. They spanned a good four or five feet.

"Is *that* what you think?" said the old man standing beside the perch. He was peeling a kumquat, and Nizaemon watched as he brought a handful of peel close to the macaw's beak. The bird snapped up the offering and then threw its head back to swallow it in a few deft jerks.

The man was Kyuzo Kugimiya, assistant at the shogunal refinery. Perhaps sixty years old, and not much like Nizaemon had imagined him. He had the air of a petty functionary and wore a long crepe silk jacket over a plain indigo *kosode* kimono. No sword, although he had to be of the samurai class.

The refinery's original role had been to produce steel and other metals, as its name suggested. But its remit had gradually expanded, beginning with research into more efficient furnaces and now encompassing all aspects of technology, including chemistry, electricity, and mechanics.

Kyuzo lived in a lonely mansion across the river from the neighborhood where the daimyo kept their second residences in the shadow of Tempu Castle. This put him on the outskirts of the city, but his high stone walls enclosed a plot of land much larger than seemed justified for a mere "assistant"—a title which seemed at odds with his manner to begin with. Despite the much larger second building beside his residence, he was said to live there alone.

The room they were in had a wooden floor and was full of strange and unfamiliar furnishings, some whose purpose Nizaemon could only guess at. At his host's urging, he sat down uneasily on a couch placed artlessly in the middle of the space. Its sturdy timber frame was upholstered with a tapestry of tiny flowers in gold, red, and green. Imported, presumably.

"Why don't you tell me what brings you here?" asked Kyuzo, stroking the macaw's neck.

Nizaemon curled his hands into fists on his thighs. "I want an automaton."

One of Kyuzo's thin eyebrows raised a fraction. "I'm afraid I don't follow," he said.

"I'm not proud of asking this," said Nizaemon. "Yesterday, I saw something... I saw a machine I could hardly believe was real. I came here because when I asked who could have made such a thing, there was only one answer: Kyuzo Kugimiya. I heard other rumors, too—talk of automata who look like people, living undetected in the city."

"So you got it into your head that I could make you one?"

Despite the ridicule in the other man's tone, Nizaemon nodded earnestly.

"What made you think that was possible?"

"I..." Under Kyuzo's cold stare, Nizaemon began to fear that he had miscalculated terribly. He lowered his eyes.

"Follow me," Kyuzo said. He turned and left the room, leaving Nizaemon to hurry after him.

He led Nizaemon out of his house and across a path of stepping-stones toward the larger second building on his property. The autumn sun was already low.

Nizaemon saw no evidence of the slightest interest in landscaping or gardening. Not a single blade of grass grew on Kyuzo's property. The yard was a plain expanse of earth, so flat and gray that it might have been pounded.

The second building was built like a storehouse, with thick mud walls finished with plaster. It had no windows, and the front entrance was secured by an extra plaster-coated sliding door inside the front door itself.

Both doors were open as they reached the entrance. The spacious packed-earth floor inside extended to the usual stone step for removing footwear and wooden board marking the beginning of the interior. Beyond that he saw an airy room dominated by a clock as high as a man. Its porcelain base was placed right at the center of the well-polished wooden floor. The timepiece itself was a three-story hexagonal construction not unlike a castle tower.

"This is an eternal clock," said Kyuzo, resting the palm of his hand on the dome of glass at its crown. The dome glowed a very faint green. Peering inside, Nizaemon saw a celestial globe marked with the stars of the night sky.

"It marks the seven days of the week, the sixty-day cycle of the heavenly branches and earthly stems, and the twenty-four solar terms of the year. And unlike a foreign clock, where all the hours are the same length, it divides each day up correctly from sunrise to sunset. Naturally, the intercalary days and months are also accounted for in its workings. It contains well over ten thousand gears, some more than a foot wide, others smaller than a newborn baby's fingernail."

Lost for words, Nizaemon could only gape at the clock. It gleamed with skillfully executed gold repoussé, and the base was adorned with masterful depictions of the guardian deities of the four directions.

"Only remember to wind it once a year, and this clock will run forever. But its complexity is nothing compared to the human body. I have attended many dissections at the execution grounds to observe human anatomy in detail, and I can tell you that to automate it would be virtually impossible."

"And yet, they say that you could—"

"Why," interrupted Kyuzo, "do you want this automated doll to begin with?"

"There is a woman..."

"Ah. A woman."

"Her name is Hatori. She is a lady of pleasure."

As if in reply, the eternal clock chimed for sunset.

II

"I trust your cricket is not drugged?"

The words slipped out of Nizaemon's mouth as he looked down on his own cricket, which lay lifeless in the fighting ring with its head torn cruelly to shreds.

"You dare to insult me?" asked the man across the table. He rose to his feet, reddening, and his hand found the hilt of his sword.

Murmurs rippled across the assembled crowd. The cricket-fighting tournament was held for the shogun's pleasure in the great hall at Tempu Castle, specially opened for the occasion.

Nizaemon stared the man down. "Your cricket did not flinch even once at the bite of my Autumn Winds," he said. "Now it continues to savage an opponent that is already dead. I have reason to be suspicious."

Despite their cool, soothing calls, crickets could be ferocious and cruel. Cricket fighting exploited this by goading two males into a fight. Some unscrupulous competitors used drugged feed or water to excite their crickets before a match; others painted their crickets with noxious oils, getting them used to the very same smell that would sap their opponent's fighting spirit.

To raise crickets in their specially constructed habitats and train them to fight by the rules was a pastime for warriors, which only made the use of drugged insects more shameful.

"Calm yourself, Nizaemon," said the chief administrator of the Ushiyama domain's presence in Tempu, alarmed. But Nizaemon could not restrain himself.

He had roamed far and wide all spring in search of the finest crickets, collecting thousands of specimens in his travels. Whenever there was a cricket-fighting tournament in one of the villages around Ushiyama Castle, he had bought the winner for a considerable sum. He had fed and watered his crickets diligently and pitted them against each other to find the best of all, on which he had bestowed the fighting name Autumn Winds.

"I will not accept losing like this."

"Then bring a bowl of water here right now!"

This was the standard way of determining whether a cricket had been given an unfair advantage. If it had been painted with oils, a rainbow pattern would soon show on the water's surface. If it had been drugged, the water would flush its system, leaving the cricket suddenly and drastically enfeebled.

A bowl of water was placed on the table, and the cricket was placed on the surface of the water.

Nizaemon and his opponent, who was from the Muta domain,

leaned in to watch closely. Officials and referees crowded around too, bumping foreheads over the bowl.

Nizaemon had expected the cricket to go limp at once, but it defied his expectations. The water rippled as it continued moving its legs and wings.

"This makes no sense," he said. "It shouldn't—"

"You persist in this insolence?" cried the man from Muta. He had been accused of cheating at a tournament held for the shogun. There was no greater insult.

He drew the sword at his waist. Nizaemon's flashed free at the same time.

But Nizaemon's blade fell not on his opponent but on the table. The bowl was sliced cleanly into two pieces. A dark patch appeared and began to spread on the red tablecloth as it absorbed the water.

"What—?"

By the time his opponent spoke, Nizaemon's sword was already back in its scabbard.

A moment too late, the men of the various domains watching the argument leapt to their feet and drew their own swords.

"Hold!"

The tournament official halted them with a gesture. "A mechanical cricket?" he asked, his voice hoarse. His hand went to his chin.

The damp patch on the tablecloth was dotted with dozens of finely toothed gears no larger than sesame seeds. At their center lay the remains of the cricket itself. It had been cut in two, but its hind legs still moved uselessly as their exposed clockwork ran down.

"I gambled everything in that moment. If that cricket had been real... Just thinking about it makes me break out in a cold sweat all over again."

Nizaemon smiled and shrugged at Hatori, who was peering into the tiny cricket habitat placed in the corner of the room.

The shogun's cricket-fighting tournament was held in autumn, and each domain brought the strongest champion they had that year. Every cricket entered in the tournament had beaten out thousands of others, and money and care had been lavished on its upbringing. If Nizaemon had sliced one of them in two, an apology would not have saved him. He would not even have been permitted to end his life honorably by way of seppuku—beheading would have been his fate. There were domains who had been stripped of all status and property simply because a retainer had accidentally stepped on one of the shogun's private stock.

"Why are men so passionate about making insects fight?" Hatori asked, smiling and cocking her head. "Personally, I prefer listening to them."

A cool breeze passed through the room. Calming trills that sounded like the rolling of a ball came from within the habitat.

Nizaemon turned away from the window where he had been sitting with a cup of sake, looking down at the reed-tangled canal far below that separated the pleasure quarters, known as the Thirteen Floors, from the rest of the city. He rose to his feet and came to sit cross-legged beside Hatori. Inside the habitat, two crickets were huddled close.

Hatori leaned into him. "Why does one have a missing leg?" she asked.

"That's the female." Nizaemon put his arm around Hatori's shoulder and pulled her closer. "Fighting crickets are all male. To calm their excitement after the fight, we put a female in with them so they can mate."

"But where did her leg go?"

"We remove one of the female's rear legs before putting her in the cage with the male. Otherwise, if she doesn't feel like mating, she might kick the male and injure him."

"Poor thing..."

Hatori gazed into the habitat with a melancholy expression. Consciously or unconsciously, she drew her feet under the hem of her exquisite kimono, out of Nizaemon's sight.

He knew, however, that one of her feet was missing its little toe.

Inside the habitat, the male had not mounted the female. The two of them were simply touching feelers as they trilled together. A warming sight, like a married couple who were comfortable in each other's company, but Nizaemon knew that the female whose leg had been removed for mating would die before long.

Who could have guessed that the cricket he had faced today would turn out to be an automaton?

The situation was unprecedented. His opponent from the Muta domain had been taken into custody at once, and Nizaemon understood that he was now facing severe questioning. He had brought not a drugged insect but an automated one to the shogunal cricket-fighting tournament. Muta would be lucky if the shogun only forced its daimyo to commit seppuku. The whole domain could be dissolved as punishment.

Nizaemon closed the lid of the habitat, put it in a rattan cage, and hung it under the eaves to catch the breeze.

He had received the habitat, along with the cricket inside it—who had succeeded the unfortunate Autumn Winds in the tournament—from his own domain's liaison as a reward for seeing through the Muta domain's treachery.

Crickets did not survive the autumn, but a habitat could be reused every year. And this habitat was a work of art, so fine that even Nizaemon was not sure he deserved it.

"There's somebody else, isn't there?" Nizaemon whispered as they lay side by side listening to the crickets.

"What?"

Hatori's eyes flew open. She gazed at his face.

Scrub off her white powder and red lipstick, he knew, and her face would be simple and plain. But she would never show it to him, just as she would never reveal her innermost heart. Even her smiles were manufactured, no different from a mask.

"Tell me the truth," he said.

"The truth? What do you mean?"

"I can't figure out who you sent your little toe to. I just want to know where your heart is."

Hatori's gaze stayed on his face, as if probing his thoughts.

"What kind of man is he?" Nizaemon asked.

"He's already very far away from here."

She spoke evasively, but he could tell from her tone that

whoever it was might be gone, but not forgotten.

"I'm planning to buy out your contract," he said.

Women were bonded to the Thirteen Floors by indenture. A rich patron could pay off the debt of a favorite and set her free.

"But..."

"The money? I could sell that habitat"—Nizaemon jerked his chin toward the eaves—"and have enough to free you and get change back."

It was the middle of the night, but the glow from the Thirteen Floors lit up the sky. Muffled laughter and coquettish murmurs could be heard all around. This part of the city only grew quiet when the sun rose.

The prospect of freeing Hatori had been on Nizaemon's mind for some time. There were two complications. The first was money. A samurai of his lowly rank could never save the requisite sum.

The second was the fact that Hatori had no place for him in her heart.

Perhaps he was too softhearted for his own good. He wanted to give Hatori her freedom even if she used it to go to the man she cared for. She would never be happy staying with Nizaemon anywhere. If he truly desired her happiness, he would have to let her go.

But that was his rational side talking. What he really wanted, of course, was to keep her for himself. To drive this other man out of her thoughts and make her his own, body and soul.

He had been struggling to reconcile these opposing urges for some time. But today's events had given him an idea for how he might solve both problems at once.

"I've decided to find the man who made that cricket automaton."

"What?" Hatori looked startled.

"I think I already know who it was. Everyone says that only one man could build something so intricate: Kyuzo Kugimiya."

The name had been mentioned by several people in the aftermath of the disturbance at the tournament. Kyuzo Kugimiya, master of automata. An assistant at the shogunal refinery who maintained a compound larger than the refinery itself, people said. The shogunate's attitude toward him was unclear.

Nizaemon had never heard of him before, but rumor had it that his work in automata was unparalleled—and that he would create anything for the right price.

"I wish you wouldn't, Niza," said Hatori, concern on her face.

"You know him?"

Hatori hesitated. "By reputation," she said in a near whisper.

III

Kyuzo snorted. "That is what you want this automated doll for? Your plan is to sell a cricket and habitat received as a reward from your domain, use the proceeds to buy this Hatori her freedom, and then comfort yourself with a replica of her after she walks away?"

The idea had seemed reasonable to Nizaemon as he nurtured it alone, but it seemed unbearably foolish to him now. He reddened with embarrassment.

They returned to the main house, where the macaw was still on its perch. Nizaemon produced the habitat he had brought with him, unwrapping the many layers of cloth and spreading them out on the table.

Kyuzo's eyes gleamed. "Well, now," he said, picking up the habitat. He turned it this way and that, examining the dragon motifs engraved on its unglazed ceramic exterior. When he opened the lid and looked inside, the corner of his mouth curled up in a grin.

"The one with a missing leg is the female?"

Nizaemon nodded.

"She's been eaten alive."

Nizaemon peered in to see the female's head separated from what remained of her body, both parts swept into a corner of the habitat like refuse. The male was drinking from the tiny water dish as if nothing was amiss, opening and closing his wings.

"This is certainly worth enough to free Hatori and build an automaton in the form of a woman, with money to spare. But do you have a buyer?"

Nizaemon shook his head. The habitat was so magnificent that word would get around immediately if it appeared on the market. If he was caught selling a gift from his daimyo without permission, things would not go well for him.

As for the cricket, it could be sold to the cricket master of a public gambling house for a considerable sum. Insects raised in domain stables were far stronger than those used by commoners. But crickets could not survive the winter. If he was going to sell it, it would have to be soon—and Nizaemon had no idea where to begin.

"I thought not," said Kyuzo. "In that case, I will take both of them off your hands. I will even create another habitat, identical to this one, and give it to you. That should keep you out of trouble."

"So we have a deal?"

"Unless you have second thoughts."

"You have made automata in human form before?"

Kyuzo nodded. "I have," he said, looking unshakably confident.

"How human were they?"

"A soul can take up residence anywhere. Use a tool long enough and it takes on a life of its own. All the more so for things made in the image of humanity."

"Surely you aren't saying that you can even give your automata souls?"

"What *is* a soul?" retorted Kyuzo. "Hair, skin, innards—I can reproduce everything in automated form. The result is incomparably more complex than that clock, but not infinitely so. What is the difference between a person and something identical to a person in every way?"

He leaned closer, staring directly into Nizaemon's eyes.

"Not even I can see into the heart of man. Faced with an automaton made perfectly like a human—one that behaves, cries, and laughs like a human on the surface, giving every impression of a rich inner life—I am sorry to say that I would not be able to tell whether all of it was truly born of humanlike emotions or simply performed by an arrangement of springs and clockwork and gears. This is a problem of great interest."

"Enough salesmanship. I want you to show me hard proof that you can build what you say you can."

"Very well. If *that* will suffice," Kyuzo said with a nod at the macaw, "I will show you what is inside it. Come."

He walked to the perch, gesturing for Nizaemon to follow, then seized the bird around its neck. The bird did not like this, spreading its wings and scrabbling its feet in protest.

"Stop that," Kyuzo admonished the macaw, struggling to get the best of it.

"You can't be serious," Nizaemon said.

Kyuzo jabbed a finger into the bird's breast. It convulsed once, as if having a fit, and then became still as a corpse.

Kyuzo unlocked the fetter around the motionless bird's leg, revealing a flash of something like a bundle of fine silver thread. Nizaemon saw that the links in the fetter were hollow and had been carefully arranged to create a conduit for the bundle of thread from the bird into the perch and then the black lacquered box below.

"The bird is an automaton?" Nizaemon said hoarsely.

"It is. Oh, the feathers are real, procured separately and attached later. But its innards are nothing but clockwork and gears."

Kyuzo held out the macaw, silent and still.

Nizaemon took it in his hands. It had a certain heft, but it was softer than he had expected. The skin under its feathers was warm, and he felt something like a skeleton underneath.

Kyuzo took what looked like a pair of sewing scissors from a drawer in the black lacquered box and snipped the macaw open right down the middle of its breast.

The cruelty almost made Nizaemon look away. A dark liquid began to ooze from between the bright-yellow feathers. For a moment he thought it was blood, but the smell of oil and the stickiness as it ran down his fingers told him he was wrong.

Once he had finished slicing from throat to tail, Kyuzo pulled apart the skin on either side to open it. The rib cage had the same shape as a real one, but it was made from gleaming machined metal. The cavity it enclosed was completely filled with gears and clockwork.

Kyuzo opened the incision wider, pulling back the skin to show the bird's innards from the scapula to the upper wings. Nizaemon saw countless bundles of fine steel fibers attached to the skeleton. Fused together like tendons, they disappeared into holes in the bones and seemed ultimately connected to the gears in the thoracic cavity. The spaces between were filled with a tangle of countless thin tubes.

"The tubes are filled with mercury to move the center of gravity. The clockwork is self-winding."

Nizaemon squinted at the mechanism inside the bird's rib cage.

Where the heart should have been, he could see a disc-shaped component. There was an oscillating semicircular pendulum like an anchor, and as he watched, a balance wheel with a hairspring struck the pendulum, rebounded, and began to rotate again.

"It does need to be wound once, but after that the motion of the automaton itself does the work," Kyuzo said.

Nizaemon was speechless. He felt as if he had slipped into a dream as he gazed down at the mechanical macaw he held in his hands.

"One of the very first *karakuri* I ever made," Kyuzo said. "Not truly autonomous. Some of its workings are hidden inside the box and the perch it sits on. Good enough for a toy, I suppose."

Nizaemon heard a paper screen slide open behind him. He turned to see a woman kneeling in the next room. She looked seventeen or eighteen years old and wore a tastefully dyed kosode.

"Who is this?" he asked.

"My name is Eve," the woman said, bowing her head low.

Nizaemon turned in surprise to Kyuzo. "Your daughter?" he asked. "I had heard that you lived alone."

"Oh, I am the only *person* here," said Kyuzo.

The woman, Eve, raised her head a fraction and gazed up at Nizaemon with languorous eyes.

"It would take years to build what you ask from scratch," said Kyuzo. "Instead, I will remake Eve into the automaton you desire." He spoke as if this were the most natural thing in the world. "We will need to measure this...Hatori, was it?—of yours. My first visit to the Thirteen Floors in some time. You will cover all expenses, of course."

He sounded peculiarly cheerful as he spoke.

IV

Hatori lay on the futon spread across the tatami mats, completely naked.

Each time Kyuzo's wrinkled hands glided over her pale skin, her brow knotted as she let out a short exhalation.

Nizaemon sat to one side, watching with hands balled into fists on his thighs.

The food and drink prepared for them lay untouched. As soon as they had entered the room, Kyuzo had produced a set of implements Nizaemon had never seen before and begun his comprehensive survey of Hatori's form.

His notes had already filled dozens of pages when he declared that what could not be recorded in writing must be remembered by feel, and began running his fingers over Hatori's sex.

Nizaemon watched from beside the futon, far from happy

about the situation but unable, under the circumstances, to do more than bite his lip and endure it.

From time to time, Hatori would shoot him an accusing look. She did not speak, but her eyes were eloquent enough as they welled with tears: *Why are you doing this to me?*

Nizaemon looked away. He had Hatori's young attendant Kozakai pour him a cup of sake and drained it immediately. Kozakai looked back and forth suspiciously between the shameful treatment Hatori was receiving and Nizaemon, who permitted it to continue despite his evident displeasure.

Hatori had not been informed of the plan to build an automaton in her image.

Kyuzo stayed in the room for three full days, not leaving the Thirteen Floors once.

He had Hatori speak until her voice was hoarse, starting with the traditional *i-ro-ha* syllabary and proceeding through a list of hundreds—thousands—of unremarkable words. He took small samples of her hair, her nails, her pubic hair, and her saliva, folding them in oiled paper he had brought with him. He had her bite down on something like a block of clay to create a cast of her teeth.

Even so, the task could have been finished in a day. Instead, he would work for a while and then call for food and drink, even hiring women to carouse with through the night. The Thirteen Floors was best enjoyed on somebody else's account.

Just as Nizaemon was losing the last of his patience, Kyuzo announced that his work was complete and dropped out of sight.

"I'm almost ready to buy out your contract."

Nizaemon murmured the words into Hatori's neck, which smelled of sweat and white face powder after he had spent himself inside her.

He had not done so in some time. He had felt too guilty after watching her rigidly endure Kyuzo's baffling and often humiliating demands. Instead, he would simply hold her, and they would sleep like that until dawn.

Before long, rumors began to spread that the habitat Nizaemon had received from his daimyo was on the market, but Kyuzo delivered the fake as promised.

It was so well-made that it might be better to say that there were now two real habitats. For a man who made automata that moved and spoke, reproducing a lifeless stoneware pot must have been no difficulty at all.

In any case, Nizaemon now had a way to defend himself from accusations of selling the habitat as he waited for his automaton to be finished.

His negotiations with Hatori's madam in the Thirteen Floors had already concluded. Her freedom would cost a fortune, but not as much as the habitat would bring. A ceramic pot worth more than a human life—a bitter irony indeed.

"You don't look very happy about it," Nizaemon said to Hatori. "I might be buying out your contract, but I'm not going to lock you up as a mistress. Once you leave this place, you're free to go to the man you love."

Hatori stared at him wide-eyed. "But it will cost you so much money..."

"The money doesn't matter. I want you to be happy."

There were stories of women who, dreading the prospect of being bought out by a man they had no feelings for, had planned a double suicide or daring escape with their true lover and been slain for it. But even Nizaemon had never heard of a man of such heartwarming generosity that he had invested vast sums in a courtesan's freedom only to let her go to someone else's side. Perhaps Hatori still found it hard to believe too.

Of course, if Nizaemon had not hit on the wild notion of making an automated replica of her, he doubted he could have gone through with it either.

"I doubt I will ever be happy," Hatori murmured. She laid her head on his chest and closed her eyes as if listening to his heartbeat.

"Don't say that," Nizaemon. A pause. "What kind of man is he? If you don't mind telling me."

"Are you sure?"

"I want to know."

"A samurai from the provinces. We met when I was still just an attendant."

"I see."

"My mistress was summoned to a teahouse by a domain liaison, and I accompanied her there. The liaison was a regular client of hers, so I entertained his deputy. Perhaps it was because he was newly arrived in the city and did not know the ways of the Thirteen Floors, but we did not sleep together that night. His innocence charmed me."

Closing his eyes, Nizaemon imagined the scene.

"He talked incessantly about his hometown and asked about mine too," Hatori continued. "I was sold to the Floors as a girl of seven, so I do not remember it very well. But it was near the ocean. There was a beach. Black pines. When I told him how I longed to leave this place and see those pines again, his pity for me moved him to tears."

"I see."

Nizaemon felt more frustrated than jealous. He wished that he had been the first to get to know her.

"Niza," Hatori said. He realized that his chest was damp with her tears. "If you really care for me, please, just leave me here."

"Are you afraid?"

Women who had been sold to the pleasure quarters as young girls might live out their whole lives there, never setting foot in the outside world again. The lady of pleasure whose desire for freedom began to waver as the prospect grew more concrete was an old trope. However unfree life in the Thirteen Floors might be, the threat of an abrupt change in lifestyle apparently made it difficult to leave.

But Nizaemon had set too many wheels in motion already. There was no turning back.

Still, he felt some concern over Hatori's unexpected reaction. He had thought she would be delighted.

Every domain maintained its own compound in Tempu, and most of those compounds stood shoulder to shoulder with the merchant mansions along Tengen Street. The Ushiyama domain's compound was in a small side street west of the street proper, not far from Renkon Inari Shrine.

Nizaemon had come to Tempu with the current domain liaison and deputy more than three years before. He had always lived in the compound with the other Ushiyama samurai, as was customary. But Hatori was not entirely unknown to regulars at the Thirteen Floors, and when rumors began to spread of his plans to buy out her contract, he became a figure of some notoriety.

Nizaemon had a wife and children in Ushiyama and could not live openly with another woman, so he rented a private residence outside the compound. It was far from spacious, and he did not much care for the smell of pickled ginger from the wholesaler behind it, but it would do.

On the day Hatori left the Thirteen Floors, he shared a last wistful night with her, then gave her some coins and bade her farewell. When he said he wished he could have walked with her along the beach of the black pines, she replied only with an anxious smile. That place was reserved not for him but for her lover, the man he did not know.

He had not heard from Kyuzo for some time and was beginning to fear that re-creating Hatori as an automaton had proved too difficult after all. But finally, more than ten days after her departure, the old man sent for him.

Nizaemon left the Ushiyama compound and set off for Kyuzo's residence across the river for the first time in months. As he strode down the street through the sticky rain, umbrella in hand, his pace quickened of its own accord. The rain was not heavy, but the drops were large, pockmarking the hard dirt road with tiny craters.

The gate at Kyuzo's mansion was open. Accepting the implicit invitation, Nizaemon ducked under the crossbar and into the yard.

He saw a woman in a red kosode standing by the entrance to the main house. In her hand was an umbrella.

His own umbrella clattered to the ground, coming to rest with the handle up like a gigantic spinning top.

The woman approached the gaping Nizaemon with a graceful tread, then crouched to retrieve his umbrella for him.

"You will be soaked," she said, offering him the handle.

Rain ran in cold rivulets down Nizaemon's forehead and over his cheeks to drip from his chin.

"Hatori," he said, forgetting even to accept his umbrella back. "What are you doing here?" His breath was white in the cold.

"I am not Hatori," she said, red lips curving into a smile. "But this is not our first meeting."

"No..."

"I am Eve."

Eve rose onto her toes, stretching to angle his umbrella over him and at least keep him from getting any more drenched than he already was.

Without thinking, as if to test whether she was of flesh and blood or not, he wrapped his arms around her.

She let out a short cry. The two umbrellas she was holding fell, and a gust of wind carried them spinning like wild things across the empty yard.

Holding her fragile body to his, Nizaemon felt ribs behind the slight swell of her breast and remembered the macaw. Her body was warm, and—whether from his own imagination or because of some component's movement—he even felt something like a heartbeat.

A curious mood gripped him. If this automaton lacked life, he thought, then what did it even mean to live?

Where was it from, the life that took up residence in the human form?

V

Now Nizaemon was back at Kyuzo's residence again.

The gate was open, just as it had been last time.

The streets were deserted this far from the city center, but Nizaemon was careful to look around before ducking under the crossbar and unsheathing the sword at his waist.

He followed the stepping-stones to the main house. When he kicked at the wooden door leading to the room with the earthen floor, the crossbar snapped at once. He gave vent to his rage, stamping on the door until it came loose and toppled into the house.

"Kyuzo Kugimiya!" he bellowed into the dim room beyond. "Are you in there?!"

There was no reply.

He strode into the house, not bothering to remove his wooden clogs, and began searching for Kyuzo. Some of the paper screens he kicked down like the front door; others he ran through with his sword.

A sudden, shrill squawk made him jump.

He turned toward the source of the sound and saw a brightly lit room. Inside the room was the box with the mother-of-pearl inlay and the perch protruding from it, and on the perch was the macaw. Its wings were spread, its black beak wide open, and it leaned toward him as if in threat.

Nizaemon strode to the bird in a few steps, then slashed at it with his sword. He felt the jolt of metal on metal, and sparks flew from the blade, but the bird was split in two from crown to feet.

A moment later, the clockwork that had been stuffed into its chest spilled out. Gears of all sizes bounced around the room with a sound like pine cones popping in the fire. Thin wires of steel bent with sharp sounds, and the bird's shriek echoed across the room. Nizaemon kicked over its box and slashed at it again and again in a frenzy until it was silent.

Leaving the main house, he approached the other building. He passed through both doors and stepped up into the spacious room beyond, where the eternal clock still stood wordlessly marking the passage of time.

A hatch about a foot square was set into the wooden floor. He pulled it open and saw a staircase that led straight down. Warily he descended to a lacquered door, and in the room behind this door he found Kyuzo.

The old man stood beside a waist-high workbench with a human arm placed carelessly on it. No—a mechanical arm, still under construction. What protruded from the shoulder was not flesh and bone but a tangle of steel fibers and thin tubes filled with silver.

Kyuzo appeared to have been in the middle of a delicate operation. Removing some kind of monocular magnifying scope that had been held in place between brow and cheekbone, he turned to look at Nizaemon.

"Not one for subtlety, are you?" he said. "Put that thing away."

Instead of returning the sword to its scabbard, Nizaemon pointed its tip directly at Kyuzo. "You lied to me," he said. "That was no automaton. That was Hatori herself, in the flesh."

"And?"

"I killed her."

"I see." Kyuzo had not moved an eyebrow at the sight of Nizaemon bursting in with sword in hand, but amusement showed on his face now. "Why did you do that?"

Nizaemon struggled to find the words. Finally, through gritted teeth, he said, "Because she looked too much like herself."

This had been enough at first.

Eve's resemblance to Hatori had been more than superficial. Her voice, gestures, and even thought patterns had been identical. Nizaemon only knew Hatori from the Thirteen Floors, but Eve seemed more than plausible as what she would have been like as a free woman.

Then, one afternoon, she said something that gave him goose bumps.

"I wonder what happened to that cricket."

"What cricket?" he asked.

"The female with the missing leg. The one you put in the habitat to mate with your fighting cricket after its match."

How could Eve have known about that evening? He saw no way to explain it.

"Amazing," he said. "Kyuzo can even re-create memories in his automata?"

He sat down beside her and examined her face closely, noting the concern in it. He touched her cheek. It was as soft as a mochi rice cake, and he saw the downy fuzz on her skin, dazzling white as the sunlight caught it. No matter how he tried, he could not convince himself that she was a creature of springs and gears like the macaw at Kyuzo's mansion.

Could she actually be real?

He began to nurse this suspicion a while after they moved in together. But there was one thing he didn't understand: how she could be identical to Hatori. Unless Hatori had a twin sister he had been unaware of, he could not see the Eve who stood before him as anyone other than Hatori herself.

When he asked Eve directly, she insisted that she was nothing but an automaton made in Hatori's image. But even when they shared the bed at night, she gave no indication of anything but humanity, to the point that Nizaemon found it disturbing.

This led him to wonder where exactly Hatori had gone and what she was doing with the freedom he had given her. Abandoning his resolution to make a clean break, refrain from looking for her, and comfort himself with Eve alone, he hired someone to search for her.

They found nothing. His suspicions grew stronger.

Without telling Eve, Nizaemon went to visit the Thirteen Floors.

Hatori's old room was now used by her former attendant Kozakai, who had since graduated to full courtesan. Nizaemon bought her attentions for the evening.

"You mustn't sneak around behind Hatori's back, Niza," she said, looking surprised but not entirely unhappy to see him. She leaned into him with a flirtatious smile, perhaps remembering how freely he had spent as Hatori's client.

But Nizaemon had other intentions.

"Do you know the man Hatori was in love with?" he asked her.

Seeing that Nizaemon was as single-mindedly infatuated with her old mistress as ever, Kozakai gradually abandoned the coquettish approach and looked at him with exasperation from under a furrowed brow.

"And her little toe—who did she send it to?"

At first Kozakai insisted that she knew nothing, nothing at all, but eventually she talked, although not without resistance. His sheer dogged persistence had worn her down.

"Hatori told me not to say anything, so you didn't hear this from me," she began.

He nodded.

"I was the one who cut off her toe, with the help of one of the boys from our establishment. I tied it off tightly where it joins the foot and chopped it off with a single blow from a carving knife. The bleeding went on forever, and—"

"I don't care about that," Nizaemon said irritably. "Get to the point."

"We put the toe in a silk-lined box and then had the boy deliver it."

"Where?"

"You really don't know?"

"Enough theatrics. Just tell me."

"Kyuzo Kugimiya."

Nizaemon was dumbstruck.

"And Hatori told you not to tell me?"

Kozakai nodded, without meeting his eyes. She had gone pale under her white makeup.

Nizaemon's hands trembled with rage. Everything fit together now. Hatori had sent her toe to Kyuzo as the traditional sign of devotion. They had secretly been lovers all along, conspiring against him.

They had swindled him out of his priceless fighting cricket habitat, sold it to buy Hatori's freedom, and then taken what was left as payment for an automaton they never meant to build. Perhaps even the habitat they had sold was just another copy and the original was still in Kyuzo's hands.

If so, Kyuzo had ended up with not only the money and the woman but the habitat as well. He must be laughing himself sick.

The memory of Hatori's apparent humiliation at the hands of Kyuzo came back to him. He imagined them laughing together at his discomfort, and his insides boiled with fury and shame.

"Were you laughing at me with them, too?" he demanded of Kozakai.

Once the wick of his rage was lit, it was uncontrollable. No one had ever made a fool of him like this before.

Kozakai hurriedly tried to soothe his agitation. On the Thirteen Floors, to anger a customer was taboo. She could be whipped for it if word got out. Nor would she go unpunished if it was revealed that she had helped Hatori amputate a toe and send it to a customer.

But the more desperately she sought to calm him with her feminine charms, the more of Hatori he saw in her.

When he came to his senses, her bloodied form lay at his feet.

From elsewhere in the pleasure quarters, he heard the strains of a three-stringed shamisen, coquettish voices at a party. He was fortunate that he and Kozakai had been alone in the room together.

He slid his sword back into its scabbard without even shaking the blood off, then covered Kozakai's corpse with a blanket, blew out the lamp, and quietly left the room.

Hiding his bloodstained hands in his sleeves, he descended the staircase and departed the Thirteen Floors entirely. He crossed the bridge back across the canal and began the long walk back to the city along the path between the rice paddies, trying not to be seen.

Looking back, he saw the brightly lit Thirteen Floors towering against the indigo veil of night. Beyond the railings that ringed the balconies, through the latticed windows, he saw silhouettes without number in constant motion.

When he arrived breathlessly back at the rooms he shared with Eve, she was still awake.

Her kimono was of a plainness he would never have imagined possible from the Hatori he had known at the Thirteen Floors. She wore no powder or other makeup at all, but her simple beauty was not diminished in the slightest.

Hearing him come stumbling in, she paused and looked up from her sewing. There was surprise in her expression but also a kind of sadness, as if she had already sensed something.

"I told you happiness was not in my future," she said.

"You're Hatori."

"Can I not just be Eve?"

Her dark-green eyes bored into him. For a moment Nizaemon wavered.

"Does it matter exactly what I am?" she continued. "Sometimes it is better not to know what is real and what is not."

"If you're an automaton," Nizaemon said, "then show me your gears." He drew his sword and brought it down on her where she sat.

Eve did not attempt to dodge the falling blade. She only closed her eyes, as if resigned to her fate.

A cascade of gears and springs, oil and mercury instead of blood—right up to that moment, Nizaemon still had hope that this was what he might see.

But what spilled from the wound his sword made was a tide of all-too-human blood.

VI

"You tricked me. It was all an act—a plot to buy her freedom and swindle me out of that cricket habitat."

"Is that what you think?"

Kyuzo had let Nizaemon explain, his breath ragged, what had brought him here. Not a hint of animosity had shown in the old man's face.

"I was the one Hatori sent her toe to," Kyuzo continued. "That much is true."

"In which case, the man she loves is you?"

Kyuzo snorted and shook his head. "I don't know where you got that idea. Do you realize where that toe is now?"

"No, I do not!" Nizaemon shouted, swinging his sword at Kyuzo in sudden rage.

Kyuzo sidestepped the blade with surprising agility. The workbench was sliced in two, and the mechanical arm rolled onto the floor. It began to flex its elbow and knuckles violently, spasming like a newly landed fish.

"Nizaemon Egawa, do you have a heart? If you do, what does it love?"

Not understanding what the question meant, Nizaemon adjusted his grip on the sword as he edged Kyuzo into a corner.

"Die, Kyuzo!" he said, raising the blade.

But then something knocked him off-balance.

He looked down as he stumbled. The arm from the table had fastened its fingers around his ankle.

Kyuzo took advantage of the distraction to close the distance between them. Then he jabbed Nizaemon in the solar plexus with surprising power using his middle and index fingers.

A hole had opened in Nizaemon's chest, and Kyuzo's fingers were buried in it to the root, searching for something behind his breastbone. It was the same movement he had used to stop the macaw.

Nizaemon felt paralysis overcome him. His movements halted. It was like waking from a nightmare and finding himself unable to move or even struggle. His sword slipped out of his hand.

"What did you do?" Nizaemon said.

Even moving his lips and throat was painful.

"Were Hatori's feelings for you too powerful? Or were you too well-made? They say that anything made in human form attracts spirits who take up residence inside it. I wonder if this is what they mean."

Nizaemon's arm was still raised, trembling regularly. Kyuzo picked up the sword and chopped at the younger man's shoulder.

What spurted from the wound was not blood but quicksilver.

Nizaemon watched in astonishment. He felt countless tiny pieces inside him grinding against each other, followed by snapping sensations.

Globules of mercury bounced off the wooden floor like water on oil. Pressing one hand to his shoulder, Nizaemon fell to his knees.

The blow from the sword had upset the delicate balance within his body. He felt springs and clockwork made of whalebone and steel strain past the breaking point within him. Other connections loosened and unraveled.

Kyuzo walked around behind him, touched the point of the sword to his back, and ran him through. The blade burst forth out of Nizaemon's chest. A dark mass was speared on it.

"Look closely," Kyuzo said.

Nizaemon stared at the mass. Its darkness seemed to be the result of discoloration or degradation of some kind. And it had a fingernail at the tip.

"This is what Hatori went to all that trouble to send me—so I could build it into your body."

"I..."

"You are an automaton, Nizaemon. A perfect replica of a man who no longer walks this earth. Commissioned by Hatori, and made, of course, by me."

Kyuzo's voice seemed to be coming from very far away.

"You—no, I should say, the man on whom you were based—had already been involved in one double suicide attempt. Hatori, the woman of pleasure, and Nizaemon Egawa, the young samurai from the country... Nizaemon died that day, but Hatori was saved."

The scene burst into Nizaemon's mind, notwithstanding the fact that he should not remember any of it. He and Hatori had put the nooses around each other's necks and pulled them tight, but he had not been able to bring himself to use his full strength on Hatori's.

"An attempt at suicide is a grave crime for a courtesan, but fortunately her owners were able to hush the incident up. They could not bear to throw such a reliable earner to the riverbanks, so they burdened her with extra debt, just when she was about to pay her original debt off, and asked me to make an automaton of the samurai who had died. I suppose they only wanted to obscure what had happened on the Thirteen Floors, but you surprised us all by settling into your life at the Ushiyama compound."

Nizaemon's vision was beginning to mist up as Kyuzo leaned in close to his face.

"To be honest, sometimes you exhibit gestures and movements that I do not remember building into you. What exactly is happening here I do not claim to understand. Perhaps, against my expectations, a spirit has taken up residence in you, giving you a soul. I only wish these things were visible..."

Whether he had a soul or not was a question Nizaemon himself had never contemplated.

But he certainly existed. He had thoughts, feelings. Whether all this was the spirit of the dead samurai Kyuzo had mentioned or not, he did not know.

"Do you have a soul, Nizaemon?" asked Kyuzo.

"Yes," rasped Nizaemon.

"How will you prove it to me?"

"If I had no soul," Nizaemon said laboriously, "it would not be about to depart from me."

Kyuzo nodded, saying nothing.

VII

"I wish Niza had killed me that day."

Perhaps because her wounds were not fully healed, Hatori pressed one hand to her chest as she walked, with difficulty, beside Kyuzo.

"I have outlived him two times now," she added.

They were on the road that ran beside the banks of the canal surrounding the Thirteen Floors. The pleasure quarters towered above them, the red lacquered railings and lattices around every floor gleaming in the sunlight. The canal itself was filled with stagnant green water, and its banks were crowded with the lowliest, cheapest brothels.

"I never thought the day would come when I would look up at this building from outside it," said Hatori. "I owe it all to him."

The marshy banks of the canal were dense with reeds. In the shadow of the reeds, swarms of water striders made tiny ripples on the water.

It was Kyuzo who had come up with the plan after the automaton he had made forgot what it was and turned up at his house.

The habitat it brought with it was indeed a masterpiece, likely sufficient to buy Hatori out from under all her debts.

Nizaemon himself had departed their world, but Kyuzo saw that if the habitat were sold and Hatori freed, she could live as husband and wife with the automaton that looked just like him. It might be some small comfort, and all she would need to do was pretend to be an automaton herself.

This was the argument that had overcome her initial lack of enthusiasm when Kyuzo had taken pity on her and explained his idea.

Kyuzo stopped at the edge of the reeds. Hatori bowed shallowly to him, then turned to leave.

He felt the urge to call after her, ask what she would do next, but thought better of it. Whatever her answer, he had no way to help her.

As he watched her walk away, he felt the precariousness of life, its thinness. She almost looked translucent.

He looked away, noticing a cricket that was much larger than might be expected, given the season, sitting on one of the reeds.

When he reached toward it in curiosity, a sudden gust of wind set the reeds rattling.

Narrowing his eyes, he searched for where the cricket had gone. He saw that it had fallen into the water of the canal, where a single frog was approaching it. The frog snapped at the insect once, then spat it out again as if unhappy about its taste.

"Not fooling the frogs yet, I see," Kyuzo murmured with a rueful grin. "So much to learn, so little time..."

He turned away and set off in the opposite direction from Hatori.

HERCULES IN THE BOX

I

When I was pregnant with you, I dreamt there was a whale in my belly.

The voice of Geiemon Tentoku's mother came back to him as he stood on the slightly inclined bathhouse floor, slapping the thick cypress pillar with his oversized hands: left, right, left, right.

The exercise was called *teppo*, after the word for the pole used in an actual sumo stable. It involved lunging at the pillar, bracing yourself with one hand and slapping the pillar's side with the other, then switching sides and doing it again. Deep handprints sunk into the pillar's gleaming lacquered surface testified to Tentoku's long years of practice and also served as guides as he silently ran through the exercise, making the whole building shake.

His body radiated heat. His back was tattooed with a fin whale surrounded by foaming waves that extended to the ends of his limbs, and this all but prevented him from sweating. After half an hour of practice he felt as if his blood were boiling.

At birth, Tentoku had weighed three times what the average newborn did. He was so large that when his shoulders got caught in the birth canal, it took three people to pull him out. When he finally emerged in a flood of amniotic fluid, it had been like hauling a baby whale aboard a fishing boat.

His mother had loved telling that story. Tentoku had lived with her on the lowest of the Thirteen Floors only until the age of five, and her account of his birth was one of his few vivid memories of her.

"Gei!" The voice cut through the damp, heavy slapping from the teppo exercise. "Are you almost ready?"

Tentoku turned to see Chitose leaning out of the tall, red lacquered chair that towered over the changing room.

Chitose was in her fifties. Once a beautiful young woman with a brisk, straightforward manner, now there was white in her hair, and the sharpness of her personality had rounded out along with her face and figure. She handled most of the bathhouse's day-to-day management these days, in place of her husband, Senroku, who could scarcely walk due to his beriberi.

It was time for Tentoku to finish up his morning exercises, bring in the firewood, and start heating the bathwater.

Tentoku nodded to Chitose and removed the *mawashi* he wrapped around his waist for training, leaving him completely naked.

The bathhouse's changing room was shared by male and female customers, without even a partition to divide them, but the baths themselves were separate. The entrance to each bath was built like a red torii gate set into the wall. To keep the steam in, the middle crossbar of the torii was set low in the frame, and the space above was filled by a wooden board with a pine tree painted on it.

Most people had to duck to get under the crossbar, but with Tentoku's bulk he practically had to crawl.

The bath chamber was dim and cool. Last night's water had gone completely cold. Tentoku used one of the rinsing buckets to scoop up some water and pour it over his head, repeating the process until he felt cooler.

He then returned to the changing room, dried himself briskly with a hand towel, tied a waistcloth on, and then turned toward the shelf above Chitose's high chair and clapped his hands together.

This shelf was the bathhouse's *kamidana* and proudly displayed a talisman from Kehaya Shrine.

Taima no Kehaya was the patron deity of sumo. In the Age of Myth, his bout with Nomi no Sukune had turned into a battle to the death. Nomi no Sukune had broken Kehaya's ribs and thrown him to the ground, but as he had raised his leg to deliver the finishing blow, Kehaya had seized it and flipped his opponent over, snatching a miraculous victory from the jaws of defeat.

This technique was now known as the *tsumatori*, or rear toe pick, and it was Tentoku's signature move.

"Always the diligent one," said Chitose, noticing Tentoku with his palms pressed together as she returned to her chair. "When's your next match?"

"The tournament to raise funds for Renkon Inari," said Tentoku bluntly. Smiling did not come easily to him. But Chitose seemed delighted all the same.

Renkon Inari was the shrine at the entrance to Tengen Street, a busy thoroughfare lined with the mansions of merchants, wholesalers, and representatives of the provincial domains. The deity Inari's festival day was the first Day of the Ox in the second month, so each year Renkon Inari hosted a sumo tournament on that day to solicit donations.

"If it's a fund-raising tournament, then women will be allowed to watch too," said Chitose happily.

Tournaments held under imperial patronage were strictly off-limits to women except for a special round held on the last day. But shrine tournaments to raise funds were open to man, woman, or child.

Tentoku nodded, looking slightly troubled. "But that's also a gift day," he said. "Won't you be busy?"

"Gift day" was a broad term applied to days that included New Year's Day, the five imperial observances, and the Ebisu-ko Festival honoring the god of wealth and prosperity. On gift days, the bathhouse plied its guests with tea and sake, and they offered gifts of cash in return. To be seen at the bathhouse on gift day was de rigueur for any Tempuite worthy of the name, so they were always busy.

"It'll be all right," said Chitose. "I can leave the high chair to someone else for half an hour while I watch your bout." She patted him firmly on the back. "Better get to work. Go around back and fire up the boilers. Don't forget to put out the sign like always when they ring the bells for the fifth hour."

"Yes, ma'am."

Tentoku walked around the high chair to the entranceway, slipped on a pair of sandals, and stepped outside.

The road was still shrouded in early-morning fog. He saw tofu and fish peddlers hurrying toward the residential longhouses and compounds.

"Hey, it's Geiemon Tentoku!" said one, stopping in his tracks.

Tentoku did not recognize his face. He stood cautiously where he was as the stranger approached without hesitation and casually slapped Tentoku's chest with his open palm.

"Look at the size of you!" the man said. "You work here?"

When Tentoku nodded silently, the man lowered the lacquered boxes that hung from a pole he balanced on his shoulder, opened a drawer in one, and began rummaging around for something. He seemed to be a seller of tools and sundries; Tentoku saw knives and planes in the drawer, among other things.

"You're just eighteen, right?" the merchant said. "Keep up the hard work and a stable'll take you on in no time."

"How do you know so much about me?"

"From this," said the man, pulling a colorful woodblock print in protective cloth from the drawer.

Tentoku's eyes flew open. He snatched the print from the man's hand and examined it closely.

The fin whale tattoo, the waves foaming down the arms and legs, even the traditional wrestler's *yagura-otoshi* hairstyle... There was no doubt about it: this was a picture of him.

In the print, he had a twisted cloth *hachimaki* around his forehead and was using a thick wooden go board (held one handed, naturally) to fan the fires of the bathhouse boilers.

A few other prints were in the cloth packet, all depicting Tentoku as well. One had him defeating a wicked ogre in battle; another showed an actual bout he had fought, with his famous rear toe pick securing the victory.

"What is this?" muttered Tentoku.

"One of my esteemed customers can't get enough of you. I bought some of the Aoiya's prints as a present for him, but this is even better. Can I get a handprint? It'll help me land a really big order."

"The Aoiya?" Tentoku was only growing more confused.

"Come on, as if you didn't know! Their prints of you are the talk of the town. Why Kainsai does pictures of you instead of one of the real stars, I don't know, but—"

The man suddenly closed his mouth, obviously regretting what he had said. He watched Tentoku for his reaction, but Tentoku offered none. He simply handed the man his prints back and headed for the rear of the bathhouse again.

"Don't get bent out of shape, okay?" he heard the man calling from behind him.

Tentoku did not keep up with every trend and rumor in Tempu, but even he knew about the Aoiya and Kainsai.

The Aoiya was a publishing house, and Kainsai was an artist who specialized in *bijinga*—pictures of beautiful women. Some of Kainsai's works were on the risqué side, but none were too explicit, and perhaps for that reason they were popular among men and women alike. Tentoku had seen other wrestlers passing Kainsai's work around in the dressing rooms before tournaments.

There was a peculiar eroticism about the figures Kainsai

drew. Even Tentoku, whose line of work had made him more than accustomed to the sight of a naked woman, sometimes blushed at Kainsai's compositions.

But now, it seemed, Kainsai had chosen *him* as subject. And Tentoku had no idea why.

II

The woman was back again.

Tentoku stared in surprise.

When she removed the obi around her waist and let her red kosode slip from her shoulders, the men in the changing room and washing area grew restless.

Her skin was fair. She was skinny and flat chested, but her lips were red and there was an ambiguity to her appearance that did not fail to attract attention—depending on how you looked at her, you might see a young girl or a woman in her prime.

Perhaps feeling his eyes on her, the woman turned toward Tentoku. She met his gaze with thinly translucent eyes like colored glass, red lips curving into a smile.

"Something on your mind, Tentoku?"

The voice of the elderly bathhouse regular he was currently attending to brought him back to his senses, and he hurriedly resumed scrubbing her back with a bran bag.

When he glanced toward the changing room again, the woman was already gone.

Glancing around the washing area, he saw her through the white steam, trimming her pubic hair with a set of the bathhouse's *kekiri* stones. He did not know her name or anything else about her except that she occasionally bathed here.

Once, and only once, she had asked him to wash her back for her. Her skin had felt peculiar in a way he could neither pinpoint exactly nor forget. He had washed hundreds, thousands of backs in his time, old and young, male and female, but there was something unmistakably different about hers.

Since that day, every time she visited the bathhouse he hoped that she would call on his services again. But despite her polite nod and smile when their eyes met, she never did.

"Tentoku, over here," called another woman as the aged regular he had just finished washing disappeared into the female bath chamber.

"Coming," said Tentoku. The whale on his back flexed like a living thing as he walked through the steam, as if swimming through the ocean in the hours just after dawn when mist still clung to the water.

Wearing only his waistcloth and twisted headband, Tentoku began to scrub O-Tomi, the customer who had called him over. Her youth had long since left her, but her appetites had not.

"I hear you'll be in the tournament at Renkon Inari," she purred. Leaning back into him, she grabbed his hand with a mischievous grin and guided it to her generous bosom.

None of this was new to Tentoku, so he shook off her hand

without comment, reached to one side for the bucket, and poured hot water over O-Tomi's shoulders. It sluiced through the slatted platform her stool rested on, then ran across the slightly inclined floor to the central drain.

O-Tomi frowned and sighed in disappointment. "You're too young to be so unflappable," she said. "Would it kill you to feign a little embarrassment sometimes?"

"Sorry," Tentoku said.

"Never mind, never mind," O-Tomi said. "I'm just another old lady, after all." She reached behind her head to put her hair up again. "You might not guess from looking at me, but I help all the young men from the longhouses through their first time. You haven't had yours yet, from the look of you. What do you say? Can I offer some assistance?"

She flashed him a playful grin. It was true that Tentoku had not yet known the embrace of a woman.

The hollow clack of wood on wood sounded from above. "O-Tomi, stop teasing our Tentoku," called Chitose from the high chair.

"Oh dear! You were listening?"

Good-natured laughter rippled across the washing area.

The clientele ranged in age from the elderly to newborn babes, and Tentoku knew them all.

He had been raised here from a young age by Senroku, the bathhouse's owner, and his wife, Chitose.

Years ago, before baths had been installed in the Thirteen Floors, Senroku and Chitose had operated a bath boat on the canal that surrounded it, offering their services to the courtesans who were unable to leave the brothel.

Senroku would busily stoke the fires to warm the tub set into the boat's deck while Chitose took care of the customers, going down the queue and washing them with a bucket and hand towel one by one. There were other boats offering washing services, but only Senroku and Chitose's had a real bathtub.

Tentoku had been born in the cheapest brothel on the lowest floor. At the age of five, he was already formidable. When Senroku offered to take him in to help with the bathhouse, his once-kind mother turned suddenly cold. "Go on, get out of here," she told him. "You're only in the way here." He remembered being ushered aboard the boat, confused and sobbing, and watching the receding form of his mother on the shore. That had been more than ten years ago now.

He finished washing O-Tomi's back, and she thanked him and headed for the soaking tubs. When she stooped to pass through the door, he saw the pubic hair and red sex between her legs.

"Tentoku, you've got a visitor upstairs," Chitose called from the high chair, leaning over the armrest. It was almost time for the evening bell, when the bathhouse closed.

Tentoku removed the twisted hand towel he wore as a headband, wrung it out, and mopped the sweat from his face.

He had no idea who his visitor might be, but despite his wariness he ascended the narrow stairway from the changing room.

The ceiling upstairs was barely six feet high, forcing Tentoku to hunch over whenever he was up there. It was a large wooden-floored room with boards for go and shogi and a scattering of customers relaxing with drinks.

"Over here, Tentoku," called Senroku from one corner of the room.

Senroku's beriberi made any walking difficult, and he seldom came out of his quarters in the rear of the bathhouse these days. He would not have dragged himself upstairs through the pain if Tentoku's visitor were not very important indeed.

In Senroku's youth, he had been a sumo wrestler too, known for his fearsome toughness. He had often helped Tentoku with training before illness had left him emaciated and gray.

Beside Senroku, a man sat leaning against the wall, looking down on the washing area through a foot-square window set in the wall. The man had his sword over his shoulder and looked slightly different from the other customers.

"Just a bunch of old bags," he muttered in disgust, then turned to Tentoku.

"This is Seijuro," said Senroku. "He's a bodyguard for Chokichi Yaguruma." Yaguruma was a minor gang leader in the area.

The man put his sake cup down on the floor.

"So you're Tentoku, eh? My boss wants to see you. He's taken a room at the Thirteen Floors. And when he does that, everything needs replacing—plates, cups, tatami mats, even the doors—so they charge him triple. He must be expecting to make a lot of money off of you."

So saying, Seijuro slid the cover of the window closed.

"If this view's the best you can offer, I'll stick to Kainsai's prints," he said.

Tentoku and Seijuro set out for the Thirteen Floors, leaving Senroku at the bathhouse.

Tentoku had not been back to the pleasure quarters once in the decade since leaving. And even when he had lived there, he had never gone higher than the second floor.

Ringed by a wide canal, the building was lit up in every color of the rainbow. From a distance, you could see shadowy figures moving to and fro beyond the red lacquered railings around each floor. When he'd been young and foolish, Tentoku had sometimes wondered what the courtesan said to live alone on the top floor must be like.

Seijuro led the way, and Tentoku followed behind. The path to the Thirteen Floors was long and straight, without even any houses along the road. If you met someone you knew en route, it was customary to pretend not to know them. But more than one person they passed said "Hey, that's Tentoku" or something like it to themselves. Even if it was just because of Kainsai's pictures, Tentoku was far more widely known than he himself had realized.

Finally he was in the room with Chokichi Yaguruma.

"I don't like beating around the bush, so let's get the important business settled first," Chokichi said, his smile kind. He was the picture of a beatific old man, a tiny little fellow as skinny as chicken bones. He did not seem to care much about his image, because he wore a ragged old kimono as if for outdoor work, and it was cinched around his waist with a rope.

Tentoku didn't know all the details, but he gathered that Chokichi's family ran the sumo at Renkon Inari.

Chokichi had been drinking with a few of his underlings in the room. Far from running wild, they were drinking with relative refinement as the women poured for them.

"You're the talk of the town, Geiemon Tentoku," Chokichi said. "If you're in the tournament, betting will be three times what it usually is. No, five times."

Gambling on sumo tournaments was not particularly rare. If anything, more people went for the gambling than for the sport. Once the bracket had been decided, the betting chits went on sale. Even on the day of the tournament, vendors mingled with the crowds standing behind the expensive seats, chits for sale dangling from their waists. This sideline, of course, was run by the same people who ran the tournament itself.

Once the wrestling was over, those same vendors bought the chits back. Whether the prices had gone up or down, of course, depended on whether they represented a winner or a loser.

The total number of betting chits was limited, and those for the highest-profile competitors were in high demand immediately, which drove up prices.

"Now, in the tournament, you'll be up against Onikage," said Chokichi.

Then I'm going to win, Tentoku thought.

Onikage was small in stature, but until a decade or so earlier he had competed in the grand sumo tournaments at the highest levels. His rank had fallen since then, but even so, if Tentoku won it would be a real upset. In the sumo world they called that a *kinboshi*—a gold star victory.

"Right now, a lot of people think you have a chance, and your betting chits are hot property," said Chokichi. He took a sip of sake. "Onikage, though... He's small but quick as a monkey. If you were to use your patented rear toe pick on him, it wouldn't be so strange if he managed to switch places with you and push *you* out of the ring instead."

Tentoku had his doubts about where this was going but remained silent and let Chokichi talk.

"Right now, your chits are at eight to two," Chokichi said. "If we work the crowds right on the day, we might get up to nine to one. Been a long time since we saw sales as unbalanced as that, and it's all thanks to you, Tentoku."

For a man who claimed not to like beating around the bush, Chokichi was taking a long time to get to the point.

Finally, Seijuro, sitting in a corner of the room with his back to the wall and his katana in his lap, made an irritated sound. "Read between the lines, Tentoku," he said, and Tentoku finally understood.

They wanted him to throw his bout. They were trying to fix the tournament.

"Keep your mouth shut, Seijuro," said Chokichi. He spoke quietly, but the chill in his voice could have frozen the entire room.

Seijuro hurriedly sat up straighter.

Chokichi's jolly expression had not changed, but Tentoku thought he saw an angry white flash from under his eyelids.

"I'm just telling Tentoku here what *could* happen. We don't need to say anything that could be misinterpreted."

Despite the softness of his tone, the room hummed with tension.

"Oh no, look at that," Chokichi said. "I've gone and ruined the mood. Just forget what he said, Tentoku, and have a drink."

He offered Tentoku a sake bottle. Tentoku got the sense that it was an offer he couldn't refuse.

III

The voice of the announcer calling Tentoku to his bout echoed across the grounds of Renkon Inari.

Dedicated to the god of rice, fertility, and industry, Renkon Inari was one of the larger shrines in the city. The approach from Tengen Street was a tunnel comprising thousands of red lacquered torii gates. From the crossbar of each torii there hung a talisman of lotus root—the *renkon* for which the shrine was named.

The sumo ring was square, with four-sided pillars pounded into the ground at each corner and a rope that ran around the perimeter. When Tentoku stepped onto the packed earth, the overflowing crowd of spectators roared with approval.

Tentoku rotated his shoulders lightly. The fin whale on his back rippled with life. The crowd roared again.

Onikage was already in the ring, which was unusual given

that the announcer usually called the higher-ranked wrestler second. Perhaps that was why Onikage was glaring at him so balefully. There was a full head between them in height. The name Onikage literally meant "deer-haired ogre," and his hair was indeed a rich chestnut brown. On his head his hair was tied up in the standard sumo hairstyle, but it also grew from his neck to the small of his back, like the mane of a wild beast.

Chokichi was lurking around below the ring like an errand boy.

A man in workman's clothes shouted "Get out of the way! I can't see!" and threw the bamboo skewer from his roasted mochi at him. Chokichi jerked his chin, and a mean-looking group of what looked like henchmen rose from their spot at the side of the ring, grabbed the heckler under his armpits, and dragged him away.

When the referee indicated that Onikage and Tentoku should begin their preparations, Onikage dropped into a stance so low he was practically crawling. This was called *hiragumo*—"the low spider."

He's not going to make this easy, thought Tentoku.

Onikage's signature move was to remain in the low spider stance longer than expected and then spring into his opponent's space from below.

If Tentoku misjudged their initial clash at the beginning of the bout, Onikage could force him back against one of the pillars. That would be a severe disadvantage.

The main difference between the square rings they preferred in Tempu and the round ones they still used in Kamigata was the need to attack and defend the corners. In a round ring, it didn't matter what your back was against, but in a square ring, when your back was to a pillar you had no way out but forward. The disadvantage was overwhelming.

In the Age of Myth, Nomi no Sukune had knocked Taima no Kehaya to the ground and been on the verge of stomping him— only to have his leg seized by Kehaya, who brought him down and sat down on his back as if riding a horse, securing his victory.

As a nod to this legend, if a wrestler fell within the ring itself, this did not mean the bout was lost. The victor was decided only when one of the two either conceded or was forced, tripped, or thrown out of the ring.

If the two wrestlers fell to the ground together, rolling over and over, getting covered in dirt but deciding nothing, the bout could easily last an hour or more. For this reason, Tempu had started to adopt round rings too, as well as so-called Sukune Sumo in which even falling within the ring meant a loss.

But sumo was meant to be a rough sport played in a square ring. If you hoped to call yourself a wrestler, you had to prove yourself in Kehaya Sumo.

As a precaution against unexpected strategies from his opponent, Tentoku decided to keep his distance. Just one step back would put him too far away from Onikage for the latter to leap at him from the low spider.

Seeing Tentoku's palms meet the earth, the referee raised his wooden fan.

The bout had begun.

Tentoku had expected Onikage to begin with a feint, but instead his opponent jumped in at him right away, headbutting him in the chin.

But they were still too close.

Tentoku slapped with his left hand to stop Onikage's leg, then drove his right elbow into his opponent's shoulder to force him to straighten up.

The dry sound of flesh striking flesh reverberated around Renkon Inari. The lotus root talismans hanging from the thousand torii seemed to sway as one all the way to Tengen Street.

Onikage collapsed to his knees, and then the ground—perhaps Tentoku's elbow had connected with his neck or chin.

Tentoku reached for the mawashi around Onikage's waist to drag him out of the ring.

And then Onikage seized Tentoku's leg.

His collapse had been a feint—a strategy to put Tentoku off his guard. He must have then decided that, as the size difference made him unlikely to gain much from a direct drive up into Tentoku's chest, he would be better off dragging his opponent down like deadwood.

But Tentoku held his ground, pulling back with his leg. If he fell, Onikage's experience in the ring would give him the advantage as they grappled on the ground. The only way the young challenger could defeat his wily, practiced opponent was to force him bodily out of the ring.

"Hey!" whispered Onikage, still clinging to Tentoku's leg. "You know how this works, right?"

The referee beside them must have heard it too, but his face showed nothing. He was in on it too, then.

Tentoku himself had forgotten Chokichi's proposal entirely.

Now he wavered.

"Gei! *Gei!*"

It was Chitose, cheering him on ringside at the top of her lungs.

With his mind distracted, Tentoku's instincts took over.

He peeled the iron grip of Onikage's hands off his thigh, picked up the wrestler from above, and hurled him toward the edge of the ring.

Onikage kept his balance for a moment, then fell forward, one leg rising into the air.

At that moment, Tentoku had the illusion that time was passing very slowly around him.

He grabbed his opponent's ankle out of the air where it floated before him. Executing a perfect rear toe pick, he let the energy of the move flow into his side, then stepped forward and released it in the same powerful one-armed thrust he practiced at the pillar every morning.

He felt the snap of Onikage's ankle through his hand. The smaller man flew into the air, landing in the audience and toppling spectators like dominoes.

The referee raised his fan and bellowed Tentoku's name.

His heightened awareness fading, Tentoku looked down from the raised earthen ring. A crowd had formed around the prone Onikage below, with Chokichi Yaguruma standing a short distance away.

He turned his narrowed eyes to Tentoku, his face betraying no expression whatsoever.

IV

"You've had an offer from the Akesaka domain."

It was just after the evening bell had rung five. Tentoku had taken down the bathhouse's sign and was cleaning the washing area when Senroku made a rare appearance to report the news.

"Ready to hear the details?" Senroku asked, leaning on his cane. "It's a thirty-koku salary with an eight-person stipend and fifteen ryo in gold as well."

Even one koku was a year's supply of rice. The offer was more than generous.

"Isn't that great, Tentoku?" said Chitose, standing beside her husband.

Senroku turned a washing bucket over to use as a stool.

"Can I accept the offer?" asked Tentoku.

"Can you accept it? What else would you do?"

"But who's going to light the boilers and wash people's backs?"

"What are you talking about? You don't have to worry about that anymore!" Chitose said, almost giddily. "You're moving up in the world!" Senroku nodded with satisfaction.

Tentoku, kneeling respectfully in the washing area, somehow felt very apologetic. He tried to make his enormous form smaller somehow.

Akesaka was a small domain in the province of the same name, but their stables had raised more than a few grand sumo tournament champions over the years. They took the sport seriously, and their compound in Tempu had a fine wrestling ring and training hall.

If Tentoku joined the Akesaka stable, he would have opportunities to compete in the biggest tournaments in both Tempu and Kamigata. Winning would mean a higher salary and special gifts, which would allow him to repay his adoptive parents for raising him.

He nodded, not needing to think twice.

"In that case, we'd better visit the Akesaka compound soon to make our introductions," said Senroku with a laugh.

The next day, Tentoku made the trek to the Aoiya. As he had half expected, there was a new Kainsai print on display outside showing his bout with Onikage at the Renkon Inari tournament.

Inside the store, almost all of the prints for sale were by Kainsai. Other than the pictures of Tentoku, all of the prints were of women—or men and women together.

Many artists produced work like this. It might be erotic or even beautiful, but with little else to offer it all tended to look alike. Kainsai's women were far more diverse.

From the undeveloped forms of girls in the first bloom of youth to the sagging bellies of the elderly, Kainsai captured the individual sensualities that other artists overlooked. These depictions all had the same calm and composed style, like scenes taken directly from life, and presumably this was another part of the reason they were popular among women as well as men.

Kainsai's pictures of Tentoku, on the other hand, were highly stylized, although even an amateur like Tentoku himself could tell that they were by the same artist. The depictions of actual bouts had the same calm fidelity as Kainsai's other prints, but the pictures of Tentoku driving ogres out or using a go board as a fan seemed more imbued with the artist's personal emotions— they felt slightly excessive.

Pondering these matters as he looked around the store, Tentoku was finally noticed by a clerk who hurried to fetch the owner for him.

"I want to meet Kainsai," Tentoku said.

A troubled look came over the owner's face. Uncertain what exactly Tentoku meant by this, he invited him into the back room for tea, apparently concerned that he might fly into a rage and damage the merchandise.

"I'm very sorry," the owner said in the back room, "but that is one thing I cannot help you with." He was attempting a stern, resolute tone, but his terror was apparent.

Tentoku picked up his cup of tea between thumb and

forefinger like a sake cup. He slurped it dry in one breath. The clerk standing behind the owner cringed at the sound.

"I'm not here to complain or shake you down," Tentoku said.

"Then why...?"

"I just want to say thank you. I can't even do that?"

The owner frowned again.

"Kainsai's prints made me a household name, which got me invited to the tournament at Renkon Inari. When I won that, I got invited to join a domain stable. Whoever Kainsai is, I owe them. I want to thank them in person."

"Yes, but you see..."

The owner trailed off. Seeing him struggle for words, the clerk took over.

"The thing is, we don't know where Kainsai is either. Or even *who* Kainsai is."

Tentoku looked at the clerk, who waved his arms rapidly in the air before him. "We're not trying to hide anything. We get Kainsai's originals through a go-between."

"Then introduce me to your go-between."

"I'm terribly sorry, but..."

Clearly they had no intention of telling him anything. Of course, a print shop wouldn't stay in business very long if it made a habit of introducing its most popular artists to anyone who asked.

It was hopeless. Tentoku rose to his feet.

Outside the Aoiya, the sky was already darkening.

It was fifty or sixty blocks to the bathhouse, a good half hour on foot. The streets were far from deserted, but he wanted to be back at the bathhouse before the sun set completely.

He decided to take the path along Ganjin Canal, one he usually avoided. It was a dangerous place by night, said to have a mugger or cutpurse every ten feet, but if he got back to the main streets before the sun went down he should be all right. And there weren't many street toughs foolish enough to try their luck on someone as big as him.

Or so he thought.

The canal reeked of stagnation and raw garbage, but it was still crowded with tiny boats. Most of them had a single woman aboard, selling her affections. Some were unfortunate souls who had become scabrous from syphilis and been ejected from the lowest of the Thirteen Floors; others were older women, approaching sixty or even seventy; still others were just brutally ugly. All offered similar services at startlingly low prices.

And, to judge from the telltale rocking motion of some of the boats, many found customers.

Facing the canal on the other side of the path was a series of rough-looking thatched hovels. Here and there men with danger in their eyes lurked between the buildings, watching the road like predators lying in wait by a trail.

Tentoku picked up his pace, but it was too late. A figure ahead stepped directly into his path, forcing him to stop.

"Evening, Tentoku. Doing well for yourself, I hear."

The voice was familiar.

It was the man with the air of a ronin who had come to the bathhouse as Chokichi's messenger. Seijuro.

"Thing is, though," Seijuro continued, "thanks to you, we took a big loss. Very embarrassing for the boss. Hardly a fair deal, I'm sure you'll agree."

He drew a sword from the scabbard at his waist. Pale moonlight glinted off the blade into Tentoku's eyes.

Raspy moans of ecstasy came faintly from a boat floating not far away.

Tentoku dropped into a *shikiri* stance, fists on the ground, and glowered at Seijuro, who stood about ten feet away. Unlike his opponent, Tentoku was unarmed, but he thought he had a chance if he could use his full body weight. He quickly formulated a plan: knock Seijuro into the canal somehow, and then run for it.

Seijuro was surprisingly calm. He must have some confidence in his swordsmanship.

Tentoku sprang forward, preparing to charge Seijuro off his feet.

But at the first step, pain stabbed into the sole of his foot.

He grunted and lost his balance, landing with one hand on the ground, and felt the same pain run through his palm.

He brought his hand close to his face and peered at it in the dim light. A four-pointed iron star was embedded in his palm by one wickedly sharp tine.

Makibishi. Seijuro must have covered the path with them in advance.

It did him no good to notice that now. The one he had stepped on must be hooked; every step he took sent agony up his spine. Running away from this fight was no longer an option. He could barely even walk.

"Let me tell you what I thought," Seijuro said. "If I were fighting a bear or a wild boar, what would I do? I even considered laying a tiger trap for you." He laughed. "Now, this is just a warning, so

I'm not going to kill you. But your wrestling days are over, kid. Lucky for you, you don't need both arms to wash backs at the bathhouse."

"Wait," Tentoku stuttered, paralyzed with pain, but he had barely gotten the word out when Seijuro's blade flashed.

An instant later, Tentoku's severed hand fell to the ground. Blood spewed from the wound, as if to paint the darkness even blacker.

Seijuro turned and fled.

Tentoku, already woozy from blood loss, curled up into a ball. There was no point in calling for help—this was Ganjin Canal. He would only attract someone eager to finish him off and loot his corpse.

At the sound of footsteps approaching, he stiffened and raised his head.

Standing before him, contrary to his worst expectations, was a woman in a red kosode.

It was her. The woman from the bathhouse.

No rain was falling, but she carried an opened umbrella, resting it on her shoulder. Tentoku looked up at her from where he knelt on the ground.

And then everything was suddenly very far away.

V

When I was pregnant with you, I dreamt there was a whale in my belly.

Somewhere he thought he heard his mother's voice.

He was in a dark box, curled up and hugging his knees.

The whale on his back began to thrash until the foamy waves that ran down his arms and legs set his very skin in motion and the open sea spilled out of him.

Then he *was* a whale, spouting a jet of vapor into the air before diving beneath the surface.

He saw curtains of light rippling in the vivid blue waters of the ocean.

"Back with us, are you?"

A male voice called him back.

Opening his eyes just a fraction, Tentoku found himself in unfamiliar surroundings.

"Where am I?" he asked.

"Eve carried you back here after she found you bleeding to death by Ganjin Canal."

He realized that he was lying on a stone floor.

The air was chilly. There were no windows or openings to let in light from outside, and he saw no candles or lamps, but somehow the room was brightly lit.

He sat up to see a man of perhaps sixty standing before him. The man wore an indigo kosode with a long crepe silk jacket. He had the air of a petty official in the shogunate, and this only made the tubelike object he wore over one eye seem all the stranger.

"Who are you?" Tentoku said.

"I am Kyuzo Kugimiya, assistant at the shogunal refinery, and you are in my home. Unfortunately, I am no physician, but I do know how to sew up a sword wound."

Tentoku started and looked down at his arm.

His entire right forearm had been severed. The arm now ended just below the elbow in a tight bundle of white cloth with blood seeping through the end.

"Now that you are awake, be off to your home," said Kyuzo. "I don't have room here for gigantic sumo wrestlers to laze around."

"Kyuzo, don't be like that. You must help him somehow. Just keep him from leaving and I'll do the rest."

"What are you talking about? You'll be stuck like that for at least two or three more days. I must inspect every detail."

"I know, I know...but still..."

Who is he speaking to? Tentoku thought warily.

Kyuzo was looking in the direction of several raised platforms. Tentoku could not see what was on them from the floor, but the voice certainly sounded as if it were coming from there.

"I hear you are a sumo wrestler," said Kyuzo to him. "Geiemon Tentoku, was it?"

"Yes," said Tentoku weakly.

"Losing a hand puts an end to that career, I suppose. You can't reach for their belt while protecting your own if you only have one hand."

That much was true.

"I'd just gotten an offer to join a stable," said Tentoku. "I was finally going to be able to pay back the couple who adopted me. They run the bathhouse—"

"Save the sob story for them, then," Kyuzo said. With obvious disinterest, he turned and walked toward the platforms.

Seeing nothing else he could do, Tentoku used his remaining hand to push himself to his feet.

What he saw once he was standing made him gasp.

In the middle of the room were six platforms of various sizes, all glowing white.

The central platform, the largest, had a woman's headless torso on it.

To the left and right of this, about three feet away, stood two narrower platforms with arms resting on them. Further down were two more narrow platforms on which had been placed a leg each.

All of these limbs were connected to the torso by bundles of tubes and wires that sagged low between the platforms.

The eeriest thing was the female head sitting on the far

platform, beyond the central one. It looked like a display after an execution.

"What is this?" Tentoku asked. The sight was so bizarre that he found himself surprisingly calm.

He knew the head from somewhere. But where?

Then it hit him. It was the woman from the bathhouse. The woman in the red kosode.

"Try moving your fingers," Kyuzo said to the head, ignoring the baffled Tentoku. "One at a time. Slowly."

He could see into the open ends of the limbs on the platform, giving him a cross-section view of their dully gleaming, apparently machined bones. It took a moment for him to realize that the incessant squirming motion was actually the gears and clockwork that had been packed into them.

The head blinked its reply to Kyuzo—nodding would have been impractical—and the fingers of one of the arms on a separate platform began slowly moving. They flexed one by one, from the thumb outward, as if testing the joints.

"Did you...*make* those arms?" Tentoku asked.

"Oh, I made more than her arms. The woman is an automaton from head to toe."

Tentoku leaned closer to the headless torso, trying to see what an automaton was like inside.

"Please don't stare like that," the head said. She never showed a hint of embarrassment when stripping down at the bathhouse, but her cheeks were burning red now. She bit her lip and closed her eyes.

Tentoku hurriedly looked away.

"Don't let her bother you," Kyuzo said. "She has the form of a human, but she is not ensouled."

Tentoku struggled to believe this. What about the embarrassed look he had just seen? Was it just a front designed to deceive him?

He looked down at his right arm. It still felt whole to him, even below the elbow. A phantom remnant of sensation.

"Kyuzo," said the woman.

"What?"

"Would you consider making an arm for our esteemed guest?"

Tentoku looked up in surprise.

"You could do that?" he asked.

Kyuzo frowned deeply. He removed the scope from his eye.

"I have never joined a human body to an automaton," he said.

"But if anyone could do it..." said the head.

"Eve, be quiet for once," Kyuzo said softly.

Eve closed her eyes.

"I suppose you know about Kainsai's prints," Kyuzo said. "She must have learned about you that way." He almost sounded apologetic.

But Tentoku was preoccupied by the possibility of his arm being restored.

Perhaps detecting that from his expression, Kyuzo spoke again.

"As I said earlier, I've never joined an automaton to a human body. My concern is that if a soul can learn to drive a machine, the machine may react unpredictably when the soul is in turmoil. In truth I do not know what might happen in that case. Is this risk acceptable to you?"

Tentoku nodded.

"Do you have money? Even for a single arm, this won't be cheap."

"The Akesaka stable is offering me fifteen ryo in gold to sign up. Will that be enough?"

After a moment's consideration, Kyuzo nodded.

VI

Rumors spread that Tentoku's troubles with Chokichi had ended in his secret murder. When he appeared at the bathhouse again, a month had passed.

He steadfastly refused to tell Senroku and Chitose where he had been. He accepted the Akesaka domain's offer, and his fifteen ryo vanished immediately.

Even then, Senroku and Chitose did not press the matter further, trusting that he was doing what he must given whatever circumstances he now found himself under. Their kindness made his chest ache.

Even after he moved to the Akesaka compound to live and train with the rest of the stable—even after he began competing in the major tournaments and rising up the rankings—Tentoku never missed a gift day at the bathhouse. And as a sign of filial gratitude, he always brought the largest gift he could.

Today was no exception.

"Hey, Tentoku!" Chitose called, leaning out of the high chair.

"Happy gift day," he said, placing a fold of paper on the special tray set out below the chair. The weight of the gift alone indicated that it contained a considerable sum."

"Are you sure you can afford that?" Chitose asked. "We thought you owed someone money."

Fortunately, although Kyuzo Kugimiya had taken the full fifteen ryo from him, no further payments were required.

"Anyway, you're here now. Why not have a soak before you go?"

Tentoku hesitated for a moment before removing his sandals and stepping into the changing room.

He shrugged off his cotton *yukata* and entered the washing area. It was full of familiar faces.

As an attendant, he had worn a waistcloth, but he had only a single hand towel to protect his privacy now. No one else there had anything more, but he felt oddly bashful all the same.

"Hey, it's Tentoku! Long time no see!"

O-Tomi waved at him from the corner. She had spotted him at once.

"You've really made something of yourself. I like to think I played my part. So, would you mind...?"

"Leave Tentoku alone, O-Tomi," called Chitose from above. "He's here as our guest today."

"Just kidding," said O-Tomi. "I definitely couldn't afford the gift I'd have to leave after getting my back washed by the next sumo champion."

The washing area filled with laughter.

Other customers slapped Tentoku on the back or chest and said their hellos too. In the end he practically fled into the bath chamber, diving under the low doorway. The light was dimmer in there, and the room was filled with white steam.

He stepped into the bath and lowered himself into the water carefully to make sure the water didn't all spill out at once. Cupping his hands, he splashed water on his face to rinse it off.

He looked at his right arm. Tattooed designs of roaring waves and foam now covered every inch below his shoulder, except for the fingers and palm of his hand.

Eve had done the work for him. The lines skillfully obscured the boundary between man and automaton. Of course, peeling back the skin would immediately reveal the dull gleam of metal.

After endless practice gripping and relaxing, the hand felt completely natural. He could hardly believe it wasn't the real thing.

In fact, it was better.

He cast his mind back to a conversation that had happened at Kyuzo's residence, several months after the hand was first attached.

He was already appearing in grand sumo tournaments, and the consensus was that his technique had changed dramatically. None of the wrestlers he met at this level were susceptible to petty tricks like the rear toe pick. It was painful to realize that his trademark move was useless against them and to watch the black stars that signified losses appear beside his name.

He was only visiting Kyuzo to show him how his hand was working, but he couldn't help bringing up his problem.

Couldn't his arm be made even stronger than a regular man's? Two, three times as strong?

When he promised to pay Kyuzo the five ryo he would receive as a bonus from his domain if he won the upcoming tournament, it was Eve who frowned.

"Isn't that cheating?" she asked, sitting across from Tentoku at the workbench his arm rested on.

Tentoku didn't understand the details of how the automated hand had been fused to his living stump, but the shining metal arm that appeared when the false skin was peeled back was undeniably artificial. Kyuzo lowered his face, peering through his trademark scope, and silently began adjusting the arm's mechanism with slim, tiny tools that looked like ear picks and powdered tea scoops.

Eve watched from across the table, painting the scene on a sheet of paper with a thin brush.

Despite Kyuzo's silence, when Tentoku tested his arm afterward he found it several times stronger at least.

Now he could push even the biggest opponent over. It didn't even matter whether he was pushing from above or below so long as he used his right hand. Once, when an opponent he was grappling with whispered in his ear, "I heard you were born by the canal outside the Floors—and then abandoned there," Tentoku went into a frenzy. When he came to his senses, his hand was wrapped tightly around the other man's windpipe. If the official had been slower to intervene, he might have killed the man. He had done this without even realizing it—it was as if the arm had a will of its own.

The machine may react unpredictably when the soul is in turmoil.

Tentoku remembered Kyuzo's warning with a troubled mind as he soaked in the bath.

And then someone spoke.

"Hey there, Tentoku. Still living the charmed life, I hear."

The voice came from a blurred human form visible through the billowing steam at the other end of the bath. He had not noticed anyone come in through the low door, so whoever it was must have been waiting for him.

"How'd you grow that arm back, kid? I distinctly remember cutting it off."

It was Seijuro.

Tentoku scrambled to his feet, setting the bath churning with high waves.

But there was nowhere to run. The only exit was so low that he practically had to crawl through it. If Seijuro was carrying a blade, that would be an invitation for him to use it.

"You put me through a lot, you know," said Seijuro. "I got branded. My wife was sold to the Thirteen Floors. They took my son as a hostage. If I don't make things right this time, I don't know what they'll do to me next. You're not getting away with three limbs this time. This time, you die."

Seijuro stood up as well. He was carrying a short sword, the blade about two feet long. How he had brought it in was a mystery.

"Dad, come on!" called a little boy from outside the entrance.

Tentoku moved in front of the door so that no one could come in and turned to face Seijuro in the narrow bath chamber.

Seijuro jabbed at him with the tip of the sword. Tentoku thrust out his right hand and caught the blade in his open palm.

The dull clank of metal on metal reverberated inside the chamber.

The sword's tip had pierced Tentoku's hand, but no blood spilled from the wound, and the sword didn't run his palm through. Instead, the blade snapped, flying back to sink into Seijuro's throat.

Tentoku heard the whistle of breath escaping from the new slit in Seijuro's windpipe.

Still gripping the sword's now-useless hilt, Seijuro toppled sideways into the water with a colossal splash. The bathwater churned and spilled over the edge of the tub. Seijuro floated facedown and motionless.

This was bad.

Tentoku dropped to his belly and fairly slid out of the bath chamber.

The washing room looked much the same as before. Tentoku saw the boy who had been trying to get into the baths before— he was naked and not bothering to hide the little acorn dangling between his legs. The boy patted Tentoku's whale tattoo as he passed, and when Tentoku turned to look at him, he beamed. "They say touching the whale on your back makes you stronger!" he said.

"Oh my! Sorry, Tentoku. My husband wasn't watching the boy, as usual." A middle-aged woman who was presumably the boy's mother hurried over, not bothering to hide her sagging stomach either. Just as she reached him, she slipped and fell on her behind with a loud smack.

Laughter filled the washing area again.

"Sorry," muttered Tentoku, the only one not sharing in the

levity. Still pale, he hurried off to change.

"Leaving already?" asked Chitose from her chair. Without responding, or even drying himself, Tentoku pulled on his waistcloth, ran his arms through his yukata's sleeves, and all but ran out into the street.

"Hey!" he heard the boy shout as he left. "The water's red! Is there something special in the baths today?"

He was finished. It was all over.

Tentoku trudged aimlessly down the street as the sun began to sink.

In a day or two, three at most, the authorities would be after him for the murder. He would never see the Akesaka stables again. And, since Seijuro had been one of Chokichi's men, he was sure to be pursued from that direction as well.

He could not even walk the streets without the irritation of people greeting him by name or approaching to touch him.

Setting his back to the crowds and making for the quieter, lonelier parts of the city, he eventually arrived at Ganjin Canal again.

It occurred to him that the boats on the canal would be an ideal place to drop out of view for a while. When he stepped onto one, it yawed alarmingly, like a balance scale with weights on only one side, and a series of waves washed across the soupy brown water.

The boat's low-roofed cabin barely had room for the bed.

Tentoku hunched his shoulders to get through the door. The air in the cabin reeked of the rotten sardine oil used in the lamps.

A woman came into view in the dim light. Tentoku's eyes flew open in shock.

He could not guess at her age, but she looked like an old crone of seventy or eighty. She wore only a flimsy underrobe, and her face was a mask of white makeup with a mouth drawn across it in crimson. Her long hair was almost entirely white, although nearly half of it had fallen out. The skin he could see on her arms and chest was covered in liver marks and pustules; she was clearly in the advanced stages of some dire disease.

"Oh my!" she crooned. "A big one! I wonder if I have what it takes."

"I just want to hide here for the night," Tentoku said. "Please."

He pulled some cash from the front fold of his clothing and offered it to her.

"Hmm..." she said.

He had thought the money would capture her attention, but she was peering closely at his face, head cocked with curiosity.

"I've seen you somewhere before," she said.

Tentoku was disgusted. Did even the women who sold themselves in boats on the canal know about him?

But the story she told him was even stranger.

"You might not believe it to look at me, but in my youth I had a room near the top of the Thirteen Floors," she said. "But then I fell pregnant to one of my regulars. I'd had the pox, so I'd thought I could never conceive. I decided to keep the baby. The overseers beat me, but I protected my baby. Oh, he was a strong one. No matter how they punched and kicked my belly, he stayed where he was. But I was sent to the lowest floor."

Her illness might have started to affect her brain, Tentoku mused. He flopped onto the moldy-smelling bed and listened without interest as she continued her story.

"He was such a big boy. In my final month, my belly was round as the moon. I kept dreaming that there was a whale in there."

Tentoku sat up in shock.

"I couldn't bear the thought of him growing up on the banks of the canal around the Floors, so I gave him to a kindly couple who owned a bathhouse. I wonder what he's doing now."

The woman closed her eyes and turned her face upward as they welled with tears.

Mouth working silently with astonishment, Tentoku looked at the woman more closely.

He had just opened his mouth to speak when his right hand began to move against his will.

It seized the woman by her brittle-looking neck and threw her backward onto the bed.

"Is this how you like it? You don't have to be in a hurry—I've got your money, so you've got me till morning."

"No," said Tentoku. His right hand squeezed harder. He scrabbled at it with his left, trying to pull it off. The incident in the sumo ring came back to him. It was happening again.

Eventually the woman began to fight back, gasping and groaning. The little boat rocked violently.

Finally Tentoku managed to drag his hand away from the woman's neck. Struggling to keep it under control, he crawled out of the cabin into the moonlight.

"Look! It's Tentoku!"

On the banks of the canal where the boat was moored stood a group of men. *Gando* lanterns swung to shine their beams of light in his direction.

Chokichi's men. They must have gathered out of curiosity about the violently rocking boat, only to see the very man they were looking for crawl out right before their eyes.

The metallic right hand, acting on its own, seized the stone canal wall and hauled Tentuko's massive body up to the bank.

When one of the men swung a sword at him, his right hand closed around it and snapped it in two before swinging like a club, blade still gripped in its fist, and crunching into his attacker's windpipe with such force that Tentoku felt the man's neck bone break and then watched him fly backward into the air, landing on his head and convulsing briefly before falling still.

The other pursuers hurled themselves at him bodily. One of them managed to bury a foot-long dagger to the hilt in Tentoku's abdomen. But Tentoku himself was at the mercy of his own right arm, which spun like a windmill. Desperately pulling the dagger from his stomach with his left hand, he tried to hack the rogue automaton off his right arm but only succeeded in raising a few sparks before the blade snapped.

Spooked by his bizarre actions, the remaining attackers fled, and Tentoku collapsed into a bloody heap.

The dagger must have reached his vital organs. The blood kept pouring forth. Everything began to recede from him.

What had happened to the woman on the canal? He dragged himself along the ground, hoping to somehow get back onto her boat, but his strength failed him first.

VII

"*Tentoku in the Box?*"

The master of the Aoiya frowned at the new Kainsai piece his go-between had brought in.

"Is this some kind of joke?"

Notwithstanding the title, he saw no sign of Tentoku in the picture. Instead it depicted a thick wooden box on legs, like a go board, with an intricate mechanism of cogs and clockwork extending out from it in all four directions. What attracted the eye most of all was the peculiar design—like a wrinkled jellyfish—that was superimposed over the box at the center of the picture. It was not erotic or witty in the slightest. It barely seemed a Kainsai at all.

"If it isn't to your taste, that's fine. I don't think Kainsai will be drawing any more pictures anyway."

"They're not moving to another printer, are they?" said the master of the Aoiya suspiciously.

Kyuzo shook his head.

Ignoring the other man's entreaties to stay, Kyuzo left the Aoiya and began the walk home, thinking as he went.

It had begun when he started sending Eve to dissections at the execution grounds to record skeletal and organ structures in detail. Her sketches had been remarkably good. Intrigued, he had sent her to the bathhouse to observe the various naked forms she saw there—young and old, male and female—so that she could draw them later. He thought they might be useful to him as he built more automata. Her work was devoid of subjectivity; she simply reproduced what she had seen as she had seen it, but that was exactly what he wanted.

Curious about what a professional might think of her work, he had taken a selection of female nudes to the Aoiya as a go-between, and thus had begun the career of Kainsai. The name was his little joke: take the characters used to write "Eve," remove a few elements—including, notably, the one that meant "person"—add the *sai* that meant "studio," and "Kainsai" was the result.

He did find it mysterious, however, when after a certain point she developed an exclusive preference for drawing Tentoku.

When his investigations revealed that the wrestler was also an attendant at the bathhouse, where he sent Eve for her anatomical studies, he realized that she was simply choosing her own subjects and decided to let her continue.

Anything made in human form attracts spirits who take up residence inside it. So they said, and he had seen it for himself many times in the past.

But even that, Kyuzo believed, could be re-created in an

automaton's workings. The mechanism for an effect he had not intended had crept into the system he had designed. That was all. He had given her free rein in order to learn more about what had happened.

An ensouled automaton! The idea was ridiculous.

Or so he had thought.

When he arrived back at his home, Eve was fast asleep, slumped forward over a four-legged box like a go board.

No. She only *looked* asleep. She had simply closed her eyes and stopped moving.

Tentoku had been half dead when she had found him aboard a boat on Ganjin Canal.

His automated right arm was missing, and the wound in his abdomen was maggoty and foul, but he still drew breath.

Kyuzo had his doubts about how diligently Tentoku had been nursed aboard the boat, but certainly he had been better off there than by the side of the path along the canal, waiting for someone to finish him off.

The box was what had become of him.

It was an emergency measure, and Kyuzo had his doubts about whether the result could even be called human.

"Eve."

Her eyes opened.

A human form without life and a life shut up in a box. An interesting combination, but were he in that circumstance, he would not have been able to love either the form or the life, he mused.

Then it hit him. If that was so, then when one person loved another, it was neither form nor life that they loved but something else entirely.

But what could it be? No answer suggested itself.

"I was dreaming," Eve said slowly.

"Don't be ridiculous," Kyuzo snapped as he sat down by her, legs crossed. "Automata do not dream."

"I dreamt I was a whale swimming in the open sea," she said, and stroked the box with affection.

THESEUS IN THE
AGE OF MYTH

I

Nakasu Kannon Temple stood on a permanent sandbar in the Okawa River. It was connected to the shore by an arched drum bridge, so wide that everyone just called it "Ten-Span Bridge" and so high at its peak that to observers below the people crossing it looked like tiny dolls.

Jinnai Tasaka stepped onto the bridge and began to climb. The mouth of the river was not far away, and he could faintly smell the ocean. Here and there a seabird perched on the bridge's red lacquered railings.

At the top of the bridge, Jinnai stopped to lean over the railing and look down. A little fishing boat full of nets was making its way to the sea. He estimated the bridge's height at thirty, thirty-five feet.

He turned to survey Nakasu Kannon itself. The sandbar was

as large as a small island, and the temple complex covered it from end to end. The bridge led directly to a path that passed through Bonten Gate into a broad plaza. Facing the plaza were a five-story pagoda with a sharply rising finial and Kannon-do, a cavernous hall with a roof of gilded tile.

An elderly woman whose dress suggested that she had traveled a long way to get there dropped to her knees beside him, heedless of the people around her, and began mumbling to herself with prayer beads in hand.

First-time visitors to Nakasu Kannon were often overcome by the majestic view as they crested the bridge. To them, it was like a vision of the paradise they were promised in the next life.

Jinnai, however, did not much care for the temple's sumptuous adornments.

He finished crossing the bridge and began weaving through the crowds around the stalls that lined the main path, his eyes fixed straight ahead.

It was even more crowded than usual today. The first Day of the Ox each month was a festival day at Nakasu Kannon. The usual karakuri floats would be trundled out, and Jinnai imagined that many of the people here had come specifically to see the little automated dolls perform.

He passed under the massive Bonten Gate into the plaza, which was even more crowded.

At the east and west of the plaza were parked two gigantic wheeled floats, each two stories high with a peaked roof, patiently waiting for showtime.

Slipping through the crowds, Jinnai made his way toward Kannon-do, where the crowds were surprisingly thin.

He stopped before a white stone pillar that stood by the path. The pillar was square, with an empty chamber at the top like a lantern. The chamber was open to all four sides of the pillar, and in each opening had been set an iron rod threaded with wooden tabs. It was the shrine's hundred-prayer stone, and each of the four iron rods was an abacus for the use of devotees completing the traditional ritual of praying in Kannon-do one hundred times on a single visit.

The abacus on one side appeared to be in use.

Jinnai looked toward Kannon-do Hall and saw the woman he was looking for.

Her kosode was a startling red, and her long black hair was pinned neatly up with a single hairpin. The nape of her neck was a hypnotic white.

Her name, according to his sources, was Eve.

She lived in the private residence of Kyuzo Kugimiya, assistant at the shogunal refinery, but it was not clear whether she was a family member or some kind of servant. Kyuzo was not married, and Jinnai had heard no suggestion that he had a daughter.

Whenever this woman had business by the Okawa, she always made time to visit Nakasu Kannon and offer a hundred prayers.

Examining the abacus more closely, Jinnai saw that she only had a few rounds to go. He moved a short distance away to avoid disturbing her and waited patiently.

When Eve returned from her final lap, she found him leaning against the pillar. An uncertain expression crossed her face.

Her eyes were like green agate, so richly colored that they seemed almost translucent. He felt drawn into them despite himself.

"Can I help you?" she asked, reaching out to push the final tab on the abacus to the end with her slender white fingers.

He had not heard her speak before. Her voice was deeper, more self-possessed than he had expected.

"You come here to pray a lot, don't you?" he said with careful mildness, as if discussing the weather. "I see you here occasionally. Got to wondering about you."

"Is that so?" she replied. She looked puzzled.

"It's just that you look exactly like my little sister back home."

"Your sister? That one won't work on me, I'm afraid," she said with a hint of a smile.

"No, it's true," Jinnai insisted. "Listen, the stalls are all open today. Let me buy you some dumplings."

"If you insist. You're the first man to approach me this way, you know," Eve said, although she did not seem especially pleased about the experience. She straightened the neck of her red kosode.

Jinnai smiled inwardly. Success.

As they walked toward the plaza, Jinnai cast his mind back to the day, about a month ago, when he had been summoned to an audience with the shogun's master of accounts.

"I am to investigate the refinery's cash flows, then?" asked Jinnai. Still prostrating himself, he raised his head to see the nod of reply from Lord Kakita, governor of Aji. The governorship was largely an honorary title, but his position as master of the shogun's accounts made him a powerful man.

"The Haga family, who run the bureau of the Conch and Taiko, order fifteen hundred ryo of public funds diverted to the refinery each year without any discussion."

"I see."

Investigating a matter that had been placed beyond discussion was not a legitimate use of a shogunate intelligence agent like Jinnai.

In other words, this was a private inquiry by Kakita alone.

"Once we find their weakness, they will be ours," said Kakita. "Do not waste your apprehension on the Conch and Taiko, of all organizations." He smoothed his long white eyebrows as he spoke, as he always did when irritated.

Officially, the Conch and Taiko were responsible for sounding the conch trumpets and beating the taiko drums in battle, just as their name suggested. The bureau had been controlled by the Haga family for generations, since the founding of the Tempu shogunate itself, but in this age of peace their only duty was attending an annual falconry expedition and entertaining the participants with the fruit of their daily practice. Or, at least, this was how the public thought of them, as well as much of the shogunal bureaucracy.

The master of accounts were responsible for the shogunate's public funds that related to matters of the stage. But the Haga family outranked Kakita in status, leaving him no choice but to follow their orders even in his own domain. Apparently Kakita found this difficult to bear.

The intelligence service Jinnai belonged to reported directly to the shogun, but officially it did not exist, leaving it without formal support. Normally, agents simply found patrons within the shogunal bureaucracy as they wished. Jinnai was employed by Kakita's office as a retainer.

Should trouble at home or abroad threaten the shogunate, all the agents were expected to gather on the shogun's orders at his residence, ostensibly to tend his Garden of August Repose. In the absence of such trouble, they had no reason to exist, putting them in much the same position as the Conch and Taiko.

"Do you know of a man named Kyuzo Kugimiya?" asked Kakita.

Jinnai shook his head.

"He is the refinery assistant."

"Assistant?" Jinnai was unfamiliar with the position.

"He specializes in automata but maintains a residence above that station. There are suspicions that he is a front concealing the true nature of their finances."

It was certainly plausible. "Assistant" was a vague position; perhaps it had been invented to put away funds in secret.

"Understood, Lord Kakita," said Jinnai.

When he left Kakita's residence, the sun was still high in the sky.

He headed straight for Kyuzo Kugimiya's residence. The most direct route was a long, inclined road lined with bamboo thickets that buzzed with striped mosquitoes not just in summer but all year round.

A fine, misty rain began to fall as he walked, which suited his purposes perfectly. The drizzle would erase his presence. He pulled his conical straw hat low and quickened his pace, ignoring how damp he was getting.

Kyuzo's residence was in a lonely area across the river from the neighborhood where the domains kept their compounds. As Jinnai had heard, it stood on a relatively large plot of land surrounded by walls of pounded earth. Peering over these, he saw the main residence and another even larger building.

Jinnai circled the exterior walls once and decided to leave. The area was too isolated and empty; it would arouse suspicion if anyone saw him lurking there.

Turning the corner, he saw a human figure and froze.

It was a woman holding a red umbrella, just emerging from Kyuzo's gate.

It was Eve.

And now he was escorting her to the karakuri show at Nakasu Kannon.

The floats faced each other across the plaza, one in the east and the other in the west. Each was about six feet high with a two-foot wooden rail jutting out from its roof and a red-carpeted platform beside it. Jinnai heard flutes and bowed strings being played.

Suddenly, with a loud springing noise, a three-foot doll in the form of a child somersaulted backward out of the float on the east side to land on the wooden rail. The audience cheered. The doll was dressed in rich maroon fabric embroidered with gold and silver thread, and carried a sword at its waist.

How the doll's mechanism worked Jinnai did not know, but as he watched, it spun at the end of the rail, straightened its back, and then seized the hilt of its sword and drew the blade. Even Jinnai cheered at that.

He glanced at Eve standing beside him and was surprised to see what looked like melancholy pity on her face as she watched the doll posing atop the float.

Jinnai's intuition as an intelligence agent warned him that there was something strange about this woman. The only problem was that he couldn't tell just what that something might be. This had never happened to him before.

With a burst of percussion, the float at the west edge of the plaza began its own show.

A large drum began to beat, so low that Jinnai felt it in his gut, and a doll about four feet tall and dressed in a monk's black robes rose from the depths of the float.

Instead of somersaulting, it plodded out along the rail step-by-step, turning its head from side to side as it went. It carried a *naginata* pole arm in both hands and had an iron club and forked *sasumata* strapped to its back. Unlike the fresh-faced doll across the plaza, it had a grim, grizzled mien, and its head was shaved bald.

When both dolls had reached the edge of their respective rails, the floats themselves began to move. The audience fell back, clearing the space between the floats as they came together close enough for the rails to almost touch.

And then the automata raised their weapons and began to fight.

Jinnai had heard that the floats were impressive, but seeing them in person was astonishing.

Tiny sparks flew with every clash of their blades.

Each karakuri was accompanied by a man in a black *eboshi*

hat who watched the fight closely and signaled to the float with a baton. The dolls must be controlled from inside the floats, each of which could fit a team of twelve or more by Jinnai's estimation.

The acrobat in maroon finally got the better of the black-robed monk, ending the show. The gathered crowd started to break up and drift away. Jinnai and Eve walked with the current of people toward Ten-Span Bridge.

"I suppose you approached me because you know that I live with Kyuzo Kugimiya," Eve said. "Is there something you wish to ask?"

This caught Jinnai off guard.

"Well..."

Not knowing exactly how far she had seen through his ruse, he decided to keep things vague.

"All right," he said, flashing a rakish smile. "You win. There's no sister. I have seen you before, though, and it was love at first sight. I've been waiting since then for a chance to talk to you. I gather that you're Kyuzo Kugimiya's daughter?"

"Not his real daughter," Eve said. She tilted her head as she looked at him. He thought he detected a hint of loneliness.

"By which you mean... ?"

"He treats me well, but he does not think of me as his child. This is what I pray to Lady Kannon for—to become a real daughter to him one day. Even though I know that such a wish can never be granted."

"I see."

Not knowing what other words to offer her, Jinnai said nothing more.

II

"Smells rotten to me," muttered Kihachi Umekawa.

"Rotten?" said Jinnai.

"You remember late last year when the Muta domain was dissolved."

Jinnai nodded.

The two of them were speaking in a quiet corner of Tempu Castle's white-graveled grounds. It was a peaceful, sunny day. Kihachi was standing on a rickety wooden stepladder, using two-handed shears to prune a plum tree now bare of flower and fruit.

Jinnai, dressed in a gardener's work clothes, was holding the stepladder steady with a foot on its lowest rung.

Guarding Tempu Castle was one of the most important responsibilities of the intelligence service, but in a time without war, they were not so much guards as gardeners, dividing their time between the occasional patrol and tending the Garden of August Repose.

As head gardener, Kihachi was on permanent assignment at the guardhouse inside the castle. On the rare occasions he came to somebody's attention, he was just a cheerful-looking old man who roamed the grounds with a broom. He made himself useful and was well-liked by the castle's maids and concubines for that reason.

Few suspected that he ran the shogun's entire network of spies.

"I asked around the cricket-fighting officials," said Kihachi, considering each branch carefully as he pruned the tree. "It seems there really was an incident at the grand tournament last year. Someone had a mechanical cricket."

Kihachi's ear for rumor never failed to impress. The other members of the service each had their own patron and pursued their own goals. Not all of those goals were mutually compatible, so few shared information freely.

But Kihachi's case was different. As head of the service, he knew what everyone under him was doing, at least in broad strokes. They all reported to the castle every few days for patrol duty, and if you asked him a question on one visit, he was guaranteed to have an answer by the next.

This was certainly handy, but whether the information could be put to good use or not depended on the agent. Not even Kihachi would reveal who else might be involved, or in what capacity.

Most of the agents came to Tempu Castle not for the purpose of fulfilling their duties as guards and laborers so much as to consult with Kihachi. Some came even more often than they were required to.

"The way I hear it," Kihachi said, "it started as an accusation of fielding a drugged insect, but it turned out that the thing was actually an automaton."

"And that's why Muta domain was dissolved?"

"Sounds like it," said Kihachi, snipping off another branch.

It would certainly have been an unprecedented outrage to secretly enter an automaton in the grand cricked-fighting tournament attended by the shogun himself.

"But that's not all," Kihachi continued. "The one who caught Muta cheating was a man from Ushiyama domain by the name of Egawa. And he's gone missing."

That was an unsettling detail.

A pair of samurai wearing long and short swords—probably stationed at the castle—walked by joking with each other, not even glancing at Jinnai and Kihachi.

This was how Kihachi worked. He discussed every topic in the same mild tone he used for the weather or his plans for lunch. The official who had spoken to him about the tournament probably didn't even remember what he had leaked.

"Now, this Egawa," Kihachi said. "From what I hear, he was a *very* regular visitor to the Thirteen Floors, right up until he disappeared. And Kyuzo sometimes came along as his guest."

Jinnai neatly swept up the cuttings under the tree, handed Kihachi a small token of his appreciation, and left the castle grounds.

Something about Kihachi's story didn't sit quite right with him. Was it really possible to make a cricket automaton so skillfully that it was indistinguishable from the real thing? He thought back to the karakuri show he had watched with Eve several days before.

Jinnai knew little of automata, but in the short time since beginning his investigation, he had gathered that most of the technology currently in use ultimately derived from the Institute of Machinery, a private school run by a certain Keian Higa in Utsuki province.

Keian Higa. Not a single member of the intelligence service was unfamiliar with the name, albeit for entirely different reasons.

Some thirty years ago, Keian's institute had freely shared knowledge of chemistry, electricity, and mechanics with all who came to learn, both young and old. Before long Keian had over a hundred students. The Utsuki domain granted him special privileges. Retainers and even daimyos from far-flung provinces sent their sons to learn at his feet.

All the while, however, Keian was forming an army of ronin unhappy with the shogun's governance and working with his closest disciples to devise and manufacture peculiar weapons of war, from guns and cannons that did not need to be lit to devices whose purposes were still unclear. He built up his arsenal in secret, quietly preparing to overthrow the shogunate.

The planned rebellion was nipped in the bud when one of Keian's ronin tipped off the authorities. Keian was arrested and executed, and his severed head was displayed for days. Most of his students met the same fate.

The institute's collection of books, plans, and automata had been seized and inspected. Jinnai had heard that this library was the cornerstone of the refinery's technology and was likely stored at the refinery to this day.

Management of the refinery did not pass from father to son as it did for the Conch and Taiko. Like the office of the master of accounts, the refinery was part of the public service and was staffed by retainers and senior officials—bureaucrats, in a word, not experts in refining or technology itself. Perhaps because of these special circumstances, the head of the refinery had been replaced twice in the past decade alone. Kyuzo Kugimiya might be only an assistant, but his history at the refinery went much further back.

Which was why Jinnai had decided to ignore the actual head of the refinery for now in favor of investigating Kyuzo, his circle, and their connections to Keian Higa.

He realized that he was walking toward Nakasu Kannon. The loneliness in Eve's expression as she watched the karakuri show came back to him.

He crossed Ten-Span Bridge and passed through Bonten Gate, but the plaza was not nearly as crowded now that the festival was over.

Heading toward Kannon-do, he stopped at the hundred-prayer stone. None of the abacuses appeared to be in use.

He felt an unfamiliar combination of disappointment and relief.

Even if he had found Eve here, what could he have said to her? Too much contact with her could undermine his investigation.

But he could not deny that part of him longed to see her again, even if only from afar.

He turned back without visiting Kannon-do, then paused at the top of Ten-Span Bridge.

On the far side of Tempu, beyond the busy streets, he saw twin threads of white smoke rising from the furnaces of the refinery.

"You wanna know about Keian Higa?"

Jinnai was in a cheap, filthy restaurant made of timbers scavenged from nearby Ganjin Canal. Sitting across from him were two men. The one who had spoken was named Matsukichi, and it seemed the question had made him nervous.

The other man kicked Matsukichi, making him wince. "Show some respect! You know who Jinnai works for?"

This was Hambei Sayama. He was an informer and sometime investigator for the magistrate's constabulary, but before that he had been a thief, a mugger, and a generally unsavory character.

Jinnai knew the type. As soon as they got their *jitte*, the pronged baton preferred by the authorities, they started shaking down their former associates with it.

Jinnai reached for his chipped cup and took a sip of cloudy sake. He despised men like Hambei, but he knew that they could be surprisingly obedient, even useful, if you fed them.

Now Hambei turned to Jinnai. "I've cleared it with the boss, so you can ask whatever you like," he said, pounding Matsukichi's back once more and laughing louder than he had to.

"The boss" was Chokichi Yaguruma, who ran half the city, from Ganjin Canal to Renkon Inari. Jinnai had suspected that Chokichi's organization might be harboring a few of Keian Higa's former students—those who had escaped beheading but been removed from the census lists, rendering them nonpersons in the city. He had slipped Hambei some money to sniff around, and Matsukichi was the result.

Matsukichi was a beggar surviving under Chokichi's protection. If he had been a student at the Institute of Machinery, he had probably harbored ambitions of becoming a scholar at some point, but you would never guess it to look at him. He was gray, defeated, gaunt; his bulging eyes looked around him incessantly, as if he were a rabbit thrown into a weasel's den. He had not been to the barber to maintain his topknot in some time, and even the parts of his scalp that had no doubt once been shaven were covered in thinning white hair.

"I'm not going to eat you," Jinnai said, filling Matsukichi's cup with sake. "Relax."

He didn't actually hold out much hope of learning something of interest from the man. If Matsukichi had escaped execution, he couldn't have been too deeply involved in Keian's rebellion, which meant he probably wouldn't know much about it.

"The man's poured you a drink!" Hambei shouted. "Thank him and drink it!" He kicked Matsukichi under the table again. Matsukichi made no attempt at dodging or protest. He only let out a low groan.

"We can't talk with you doing that," Jinnai said softly. "Could you give us a minute?"

Hambei made a face but then picked up a bottle of sake from the tabletop and went to bother the dangerous-looking group huddled around the next table.

"Sorry about that," Jinnai said to Matsukichi. "Look, this isn't a formal inquiry. I just heard you were at the Institute of Machinery, and I was hoping you could tell me what it was like there."

Matsukichi was momentarily distracted by Hambei and the

men at the next table shouting at each other, but Jinnai willed himself to ignore it, not even turning to look.

"And you're...with the magistrates?" asked Matsukichi.

"No. I can't tell you who I work for, but I'm just doing a little investigating around a certain situation."

The next table sounded on the verge of either an all-out brawl or weapons being drawn. Then it abruptly fell silent. Hambei must have flashed his jitte. Jinbei glanced over to see the group of toughs sitting back down. They looked disgusted. Hambei was smirking.

Provoke people intentionally, reveal the jitte at the last moment, and then force them to take you out on the town as their treat. Not an uncommon hobby among the magistrates' informants, but eventually men like that made one too many enemies and were found floating facedown in Ganjin Canal. Jinnai had seen it many times, but he found it difficult to muster much concern for Hambei. Plenty more where he came from.

"I'm not an expert or anything," Jinnai said, "but I hear that today's karakuri are all based on Keian's designs."

By now Hambei was forcing the men to keep his cup full as he regaled them with tales of his exploits as a hired thieftaker.

After considering Jinnai's questions, Matsukichi began, haltingly, to speak.

"The incident happened less than a month after I moved into the institute," he said.

Inwardly, Jinnai sighed. The man had gotten caught up in events before he could even learn what they were. He sympathized with Matsukichi's ill fortune, but this meeting with him was probably a waste of time.

"'The mechanism's workings are obscure,'" muttered Matsukichi.

"What was that?" Jinnai said.

But he was drowned out by Hambei guffawing at the next table. His captive audience forced a thin chuckle too.

"I said *shut up!*"

Jinnai usually avoided speaking too bluntly to fools like Hambei, finding politeness a more effective way to remind them who was in charge, but Hambei's antics had driven him past his limit.

Apparently he had spoken more sharply than even he realized. Hambei wilted visibly, and the atmosphere at his table became as cool as the sake at a funeral vigil.

Jinnai turned back to Matsukichi. "I didn't quite catch that. Could you repeat it?"

Matsukichi took a deep breath to calm his nerves first. "Master Keian was invited by the imperial household to investigate the Sacred Vessel from the Age of Myth."

"Oh?"

This was interesting. Jinnai knew vaguely that the Sacred Vessel was a symbol of imperial authority handed down from empress to empress since time immemorial, but what it was exactly he had no idea.

"When he talked about it—the Vessel—that's what he would always say. 'The mechanism's workings are obscure.'"

"So the Sacred Vessel is some kind of machine?"

"I don't know."

"Another drink?"

Jinnai called to a severely pockmarked waitress and had her bring them a new bottle. Matsukichi's cup was far from empty, but he reached to refill it anyway.

When Matsukichi saw Jinnai tilting the bottle, he grabbed his cup and drained it in one gulp. Hambei pointed and laughed at this, for whatever reason, but fell silent at a sharp glare from Jinnai.

"Once or twice a month, Master Keian was summoned to the palace in Kamigata. The other students told me that his automata were based on what he learned inspecting the Sacred Vessel."

Once every sixty years, when the calendar completed another sexagenary cycle, the entire palace was rebuilt at a new location. "Kamigata," literally "the upper region," was the imperial word for wherever the palace currently stood. The last relocation had been around thirty years ago.

Imperial succession had gone through the female line since ancient times, but, mysteriously, no daughters had been born to the family for many years, as if it was cursed to bear only sons. Until the accession of the current empress, there had even been talk of ceding the throne to the daughter of the most closely related prince. And now the current empress was ill herself and rarely appeared before anyone.

Jinnai's investigation into Kyuzo Kugimiya and the dissolution of the Muta domain was heading in some very odd directions.

If the refinery had inherited the Institute of Machinery's secret knowledge of automata, perhaps that included something the imperial household, too, would prefer to keep quiet.

If so, this was a dangerous assignment. It might go far beyond the flow of public funds or political dealings within the tight-fisted shogunate, as Kakita suspected.

Beyond the refinery, beyond Kyuzo, who was still a cipher in any case, Jinnai sensed something dark and bottomless. The involvement of the Conch and Taiko also bothered him.

"'The mechanism's workings are obscure.'"

He muttered it to himself, without thinking. The words sounded like an incantation.

What kind of automaton was beyond the understanding even of a genius like Keian Higa?

"The Muta domain, its dissolution—did that have something to do with Master Keian?" asked Matsukichi.

The question surprised Jinnai. "What do you mean?"

Matsukichi looked flustered. "I just mean... Well, the ronin who leaked Keian's plans to the shogunate was later made a Muta samurai, wasn't he?"

He lowered his face and looked up at Jinnai as he spoke, watching to see how the other would react.

Jinnai's mind was racing. He had been trying to find out where the Muta domain had gotten a mechanical cricket. What if the replacement had been done without their knowledge?

From what Jinnai had heard, when the accusation of tampering with the insect had been made at the tournament, the entrant from Muta had placed the cricket on the cup of water with absolute confidence, freely inviting the referees and officials to make their inspection. But what if he had been set up by someone seeking to destroy the Muta domain?

For example, a former student of Keian Higa?

Jinnai stood up. "You've given me a lot to think about," he said. "Thanks."

He left the restaurant without looking back.

III

Kyuzo Kugimiya, refinery assistant.

Eve, the woman who lived in his residence.

Keian Higa's plot against the shogun. The Muta domain's dissolution.

And the Sacred Vessel from the Age of Myth, passed down the imperial line...

A simple investigation into where the refinery directed its funding was turning up one new mystery after another.

The mechanism's workings are obscure.

The question of the Sacred Vessel's true nature intrigued him most. Despite Keian Higa's plot against the shogunate, it had been his work that made automata so widespread today.

Jinnai had a hunch that the Sacred Vessel itself had inspired Keian's plot. The man had been a scholar from the merchant class, not a warrior. The secret might lie in the devices and diagrams confiscated from his institute.

Perhaps Jinnai would have to pay an undetected visit to the refinery.

If Keian's automata had been derived from the Sacred Vessel, they could be viewed as imperial secrets leaked to the wider world.

Whether that would be evident to a nonspecialist was another question. Even if Jinnai could catch a glimpse of it, would he understand what he saw? It was impossible to say in advance.

As he made his way to Kakita's residence at the top of Nekojizo Hill, Jinnai considered what to include in his report.

None of these new revelations were the answers Kakita sought. Instead of clarifying the flow of funds, Jinnai had only found hints at further secrets lying just beyond his grasp.

The sun had set, and night had fallen. Jinnai climbed the hill without getting out of breath. Looking up, he noticed that it was a new moon. No wonder the street felt even darker than usual.

He arrived at Kakita's mansion and was about to announce himself when he realized something was wrong. Warily, he backed off the property and went around to the rear.

As far as he could see from the outside, there were no lights burning in the house at all. He slipped into the back garden through a gap in the hedge and tried the kitchen door. It was unlocked and slid easily to the side.

Entering the dark entryway, he saw a person lying facedown in front of the cooking stove. Probably a maid. No need to check if she was alive. Her clothing was dark with blood.

He stepped up out of the kitchen as if fleeing the stink of gore, but if anything it was stronger farther inside the house.

That isn't just one or two murders, his intuition whispered to him. *Could the whole household have been slaughtered?*

He headed for Kakita's library and pulled aside the sliding screen.

Jinnai was no stranger to violence, but even he blanched at what he saw.

The corpse of Lord Kakita, governor of Aji, lay in the dwindling light of a standing paper lantern. His body faced the floor, but his eyes gazed at the ceiling. His head had been all but severed and was connected to his neck by only a thin flap of skin. Perhaps the murderer had wanted to make sure. Plumes of blood had stained not just the floor but also the white plaster walls and even the roof.

Probably not the work of a burglar.

Inspecting the wound, Jinnai found that Kakita's throat had been cut in a single blow, delivered from behind. Not the kind of feat just anyone could pull off. He doubted Kakita had even had time to scream.

Going by the intensity of the reek of blood, more than two hours had passed since the murder. And since no one in the neighborhood had raised the alarm, every single person in the house must have been killed. Methodically, room by room, with no one given a chance to escape.

Not unlike the way his fellow spies handled such matters.

He put his hand to his chin and thought. Why had Kakita been killed? All that came to mind was the matter that Jinnai was currently nosing around in. Perhaps someone had started their own investigation of the master of account's menacing actions. Kihachi was unlikely to tell him if so.

Someone pounded on the front door, then yelled in a familiar voice.

"This is Hambei Sayama on the authority of the western magistrate's office! We have received a report and are here to investigate! If nobody answers, we will force our way in to inspect the premises!"

It was a setup, then.

Holding his breath, Jinnai rose silently to his feet.

The timing was too good. Whoever it was must have waited until Jinnai was heading for Kakita's mansion before making their report.

To judge from the noises outside, Hambei had brought a dozen or more men from the constabulary with him. And to judge by the tension in his voice, he expected to find a murder scene or worse.

The master of accounts was a key shogunate official. Hambei and the others must have come from the nearest police station to contain the scene, but dozens of reinforcements from the magistrate's office would be on their way at that very moment.

If Jinnai revealed himself, he would become the prime suspect for the murders. They certainly would not just let him go.

In cases like this, an informant like Hambei had one job: to watch the scene until the real police arrived, making sure that not even a stray cat got out. But Hambei, perhaps hoping to make a name for himself, seemed to have come up with the foolish idea of entering the house and searching it himself. If the killers were still inside and he could capture them before the constabulary arrived, it would be quite a coup.

The front door rattled open. The first few men inside groaned and retched at the stench of blood.

If Hambei had any sense at all, he would have posted men at the back door too.

Hambei and his men were pouring in, shouting with false bravado. Time to make a decision.

Jinnai kicked over the lantern.

As its remaining oil spilled onto the floor, its last flickering scrap of wick bloomed into rapidly spreading flames.

Once the library filled with smoke, Jinnai drew the sword at his waist and leapt out of the room.

The men were already in the corridor.

"Y—you?!" Hambei stuttered with shock.

Without hesitating, without mercy, Jinnai brought down his sword.

Hambei tried to catch the blade with the fork in his jitte but only managed to deflect it. This was probably the first time he'd ever used it for anything other than extorting other criminals.

Taking advantage of Hambei's reflexive flinch, Jinnai kicked him firmly in the chest. Hambei fell backward, knocking over the men behind him like dominoes.

Before the flames rose any higher, Jinnai turned and fled, retracing his steps to the back entrance. Instead of opening the door, he hurled himself at it bodily, smashing through the timber and flying out into the yard.

He quickly brought up his sword in a defensive stance, but it seemed that Hambei was an even bigger fool than he looked. There was only one man guarding the door. Hambei must have used almost every man he had to storm the front door, like a bunch of bandits.

The lone guard's eyes went wide as he saw Jinnai smash through the door. Jinnai raised his sword and brought the blunt edge down right on the man's throat.

The man groaned and collapsed where he stood.

Jinnai swept him up over one shoulder and carried him to a nearby thicket of bamboo, where he quickly stripped the man and exchanged clothes with him. This was why he had not used the sharp edge of his blade: he had not wanted the clothes to be torn or spattered with blood.

He pulled the man's headband tight around his forehead, then rolled up his kimono hem and tucked it into the obi around his waist, the way the muscle at the police station did.

The fire had spread to most of the building now. The air was filling with dense smoke.

Jinnai pressed the point of his sword against the still-unconscious guard, then drove it in to finish him off. Then he slipped out of the bamboo thicket from the other side into Nekojizo Street.

As expected, several bobbing police lanterns were already climbing the hill.

Hambei and his men were nowhere to be seen. They were probably panicking back at the mansion—the building they were supposed to secure had gone up in flames.

Jinnai ran down the hill, waving both hands at the lanterns.

"Fire!" he cried, trying to sound as panicky as possible. "Fire at Lord Kakita's mansion!"

He saw that the man closest to him was wearing the leather jacket and hat of a fire brigade member.

"Hurry!" he yelled. "Please hurry!"

He stepped aside to let the man and the dozens with him pass, waving his arms and raving to inflame the situation further. As he watched them race up the hill toward the smoke and flames, he allowed himself an exhalation of relief, then bolted down the hill and away from the scene.

IV

A few days after Lord Kakita's mansion burned down, the magistrate's office announced that Jinnai was wanted for his murder.

To an extent Jinnai had been resigned to this, but it did mean he could no longer visit Kihachi in the castle gardens.

Both murder and frame-up had to be related to the refinery investigation. But the fact was that Jinnai still knew next to nothing about the matter.

Still, someone had killed Kakita to keep him quiet, and Jinnai was determined to figure out what they were hiding. Under the circumstances, that information would give him more cards to play. It would probably also help him figure out what to do next. If he was going to surrender to the magistrate and reveal all, that could wait.

After a few days staking out the hundred-prayer stone at

Nakasu Kannon, he finally saw Eve again. It was the first Day of the Ox of the new month—the same festival day of their first meeting, when they had seen the karakuri show.

Jinnai was sitting on the banks of the Okawa, fishing line in the water and conical sedge hat on his head to deflect suspicion as he closely watched the crowds crossing Ten-Span Bridge. He recognized Eve's red kosode immediately.

He waited a few beats, then set his fishing pole down and crossed the bridge after her. When he arrived at the hundred-prayer stone, he found the abacus in use, as expected.

Glancing toward Kannon-do Hall, he saw glimpses of Eve's kosode through the crowds. She would be back. He just had to wait.

He pulled the brim of his hat lower and took up a position a short distance from the pillar. Finally he heard the sound of geta clogs scraping through the gravel. A woman's footsteps.

Slender white fingers pushed a tag on the abacus to one side.

Jinnai seized her wrist.

"You're coming with me," he said.

Eve was a full head shorter than him, so the hat did not hide his face from her. She showed no sign of distress but only frowned and cocked her head to one side.

"Are you the samurai I met here once before?" she asked with a suspicious look.

She was right to be wary, of course. He had not looked like this at their last meeting; he had dressed and even carried himself differently.

Jinnai pulled the front fold of his kimono to one side for a moment, giving Eve—and only Eve—a glimpse of the dagger inside.

Eve nodded slightly and went with him, still not seeming particularly taken aback.

Jinnai led her back toward the bridge.

"Not going to try and run?" Jinnai asked, prodding the small of her back with the dagger hidden under his clothing.

No one around them noticed. Children clutching pinwheels and candy from the stalls at the temple ran past, calling for their parents to hurry up.

"I suppose you have something to talk to me about?" Eve said, without stopping or turning her head. "I have questions for you too."

Her tone, for some reason, gave Jinnai chills.

His plan had been to take her back to the cheap lodging house where he had gone to ground, but she had taken charge.

She was walking not toward the bridge but away from the main path, toward the edge of the island. They arrived at a quiet corner with a row of tiny subshrines surrounded by a stone fence. The black pines growing on the sandy shore made the area cool and shady.

In stark contrast to Kannon-do, this area was deserted apart from a single cat curled up in the sun on top of a crumbling stone lantern.

Eve passed through the torii gate into the fenced-in area, then took a seat on a convenient stone by the miniature shrines. They were crammed together like men in one of the city's longhouses: Inari, Hachiman, Kehaya.

Jinnai resheathed his dagger for the time being but stood with his back to the gate to prevent Eve from fleeing.

"You said you had something to ask me," he said.

145

"What is your interest in Kyuzo Kugimiya?"

"You noticed?" Jinnai frowned.

"I noticed the first time you approached me here."

So that was why she had talked to him so readily. She had been feeling him out even as he investigated her.

"It will only make trouble for you," she added, looking at him from under her lashes. She sounded as if she meant it as a sincere warning.

"It already has," said Jinnai wryly. "My patron was murdered, and I'm the prime suspect. All right, let me get to the point. What is Kyuzo's relationship to Keian Higa?"

For a moment, Eve's eyes of green agate seemed to look into his soul. Then she looked away, turning to the Okawa River.

"Could you swim this river?" she asked.

"No idea," Jinnai said warily. Where was this going?

"Let's suppose you could. Could you then swim back across the same river?"

"What are you trying to say?" Jinnai's confusion gave way to irritation.

"No one can cross the same river twice," Eve said, meeting his eyes again and holding his gaze. "'Okawa' only names the form. The water itself flows ever out to sea. Today's Okawa might look like yesterday's, but in fact nothing of yesterday's flow remains. So—where is the Okawa itself?"

"Well..." Jinnai trailed off.

Eve rose to her feet and dusted off the seat of her kosode, giving him a sidelong glance. "The magistrate's office, the Conch and Taiko, the master of accounts—none of them understand the situation they find themselves in. And neither do you."

As she stepped forward, Jinnai stepped back.

He gripped the hilt of his dagger, but he felt deeply uneasy about his chances with this slender young woman. He had never felt this way before.

"I am going home," Eve said. "Please step aside."

Jinnai had no choice but to do as she asked.

Eve nodded politely as she passed him, then walked away with her refined gait.

Jinnai realized that his entire body was drenched in cold sweat.

V

That night, Jinnai scaled the high walls around the shogunal refinery, dressed in the close-fitting black garb of a shinobi.

A smear of red floated in the darkness ahead—molten iron visible through the furnace's chute. Dormitories stood at the base of the chimneys, and under their eaves he saw the indistinct forms of the engineers and laborers who worked in shifts to keep the refinery running all day and all night.

The security here was even lighter than he had expected. Most of the premises were taken up by the refinery itself, so absent special circumstances like Jinnai's, there was no reason to break in.

Instead of making straight for the refinery and the dormitories, he headed in the other direction, toward the residence of the refinery chief.

None of them understand the situation they find themselves in.

What had Eve meant by this? He couldn't shake the feeling that he was missing something. Something important.

Lord Kakita had been interested only in the refinery chief's finances.

The magistrate's office, too, was likely motivated solely by the sincere if mistaken belief that Jinnai had murdered Kakita.

What was still unknown? The goals of the master of the Conch and Taiko. The aims of the refinery chief. The truth about Kyuzo and Eve.

But investigating the Conch and Taiko on his own was a daunting prospect. This left him with one realistic option: to break into the refinery chief's residence and search the books confiscated from Keian Higa for information about the Sacred Vessel.

Whether he could identify the documents was an open question, of course. Even if they were placed right in front of him, he still might not understand what they said. And he did not have much time.

Compared to the furnace and dormitories, the area around the refinery chief's residence was quiet. The residence was a fine mansion, complete with tiled roof, and had a fireproof earthen storehouse to one side. If the institute's library were here, that was where it would be.

Jinnai saw no guards. In fact, the area felt deserted. Still, he approached the storehouse with caution, then picked the padlock, cracked open the door, and slipped inside.

Standing in the darkness, he produced a tube containing a live coal and used it to light a candle he had also brought with him.

Vindication—the storehouse was full of books. The walls had been lined with shelves almost to the ceiling, and every shelf was piled high with books.

Not unexpectedly, the sheer size of the library was overwhelming. His chances of picking out the right volume in just one night with nothing to go on were minimal.

No point worrying about that now, though. If necessary, he would just have to break in again to continue his search. And again, and again.

Starting from one end of the shelves, Jinnai began checking the titles written on the bottom edge of each book. This task alone might take the whole night.

He scanned the shelves doggedly for a full two hours, hammering each title into his head whether he understood it or not, just in case.

Then his attention seized on a volume placed unassumingly on a middle shelf.

The Mechanism's Workings Are Obscure. There on its bottom edge were Matsukichi's words. The words that represented the Sacred Vessel.

Jinnai pulled the book from the shelf. The same phrase was written on its cover. He flipped through the pages quickly. There was no introduction. Just plans and schematics from the very first page.

Jinnai gasped. "It can't be," he muttered.

Some of the pages had detailed measurements and other written notations as well as diagrams, but nowhere did the book say what exactly the plans were for.

It did not need to. And the lack of any commentary only added to the ominous feel of the work.

The mechanism's workings are obscure. If he had not heard this phrase, Jinnai doubted the book would have stood out to him among the others. Certainly he would not have understood what it contained.

His hands trembled as he turned the page.

Who else knew about this, outside the imperial family?

If the master of the Conch and Taiko had kept the truth to himself, terrible things were afoot.

Was it to protect this secret that Keian Higa had plotted his coup?

Ideas that had been fragmentary and disconnected snapped together in his mind like a child's puzzle.

One thing was clear: a visit to Kyuzo Kugimiya was in order.

Jinnai tucked the book into the front fold of his clothing. If the theft were discovered, no excuse would save his life—but the same was true of simply having learned the secret. His nature would not let him rest until he had followed the trail as far as it went.

Jinnai emerged from the storehouse, refastened the padlock just as it had been, and left the refinery premises at a run.

VI

As he made his way to Kyuzo's residence across the river from the merchant houses and domain compounds, Jinnai wondered if the magistrates had put it under surveillance, but he saw no sign of that when he arrived.

Tense and watchful, he stepped through Kyuzo's gate.

Eve was standing outside in her red kosode, as if she had foreseen his visit.

She bowed deeply. "We have been waiting for you," she said.

Saying nothing, Jinnai followed her into the house. Eve showed him to an inner chamber, then went to summon Kyuzo.

Many of the furnishings in the room were unfamiliar to him. He did not even know what some of them were for.

There was an exotic bird in one corner—a macaw, was it?—with brilliant blue and yellow coloring. It was chained to a branch that protruded from a four-foot black lacquer box with mother-of-pearl inlay, and it pecked at its wings with apparent boredom as it sat on its perch.

There was also a four-legged box shaped like a go board. Drawn on its surface in practiced brushwork was a fin whale raising foaming waves. Jinnai pulled it closer and sat down on it to wait.

Unable to relax, he touched the book he had stolen from the refinery, now hidden in the front fold of his clothing. Where should his conversation with Kyuzo begin? He still wasn't sure.

He heard people approaching the room and turned to watch the entrance. The sliding paper screen opened, and Eve showed herself again. Behind her stood two men.

As soon as she saw Jinnai, she opened her mouth wide and shrieked. She ran across the room and hurled herself at him.

Jinnai fell off his seat onto the floor, utterly baffled. Eve crouched and embraced the box, then turned to glare at him. "This is not a stool!" she said. "Please don't sit on it!"

The older of the two men standing in the doorway spoke, not sounding amused. "I don't believe we've met before. Jinnai Tasaka, was it?"

Jinnai got to his feet with some embarrassment.

Beside him, Eve was muttering darkly as she polished the box with her sleeve.

"I am Kyuzo Kugimiya," continued the man. "I think you know my other guest."

Even with this introduction, Jinnai could not place the slightly built other man right away. He looked closer at his face before finally realizing that it was Matsukichi, former live-in student

154

at the Institute of Machinery, now a beggar under Chokichi Yaguruma's protection.

The broken, fearful man that Jinnai had met was all but invisible. This Matsukichi was smartly dressed and held his head high, meeting Jinnai's gaze with a smirk.

"Eve, leave us," said Kyuzo.

She did, carrying the box out of the room with her. Still not over Jinnai having used it as a stool, clearly.

"Now, we reached this point the long way around, but..."

Kyuzo gestured for Jinnai to sit in one of his exotic imported chairs, pulling one closer for himself as well. Matsukichi did the same.

"I assume you're here because you found Keian's book," Matsukichi said.

Jinnai, on the other hand, still had no idea why Matsukichi was there. He fixed them both with a glare as he replied, "I have some questions for you first."

"No doubt," said Kyuzo, nodding.

Jinnai took a deep breath to still his emotions before speaking again.

"The empress in the palace isn't human, is she?"

Silence followed, as if time had stopped.

Then Matsukichi laughed, and Kyuzo did too, chuckling quietly despite himself.

"What's the joke?" said Jinnai irritably.

"Well done," said Matsukichi. "You're the first one of the shogun's spies to get this far."

He really was nothing like the man Hambei had brought to that dingy restaurant. No wonder Jinnai hadn't recognized him.

"Who are you really?" asked Jinnai.

"A spy for the Conch and Taiko. I can't give you my name. Matsukichi will do."

Jinnai was dumbstruck. Apart from Kihachi Umekawa, none of the spies were supposed to know what their fellow spies were investigating.

"So that story about the Institute of Machinery, and your arrest and expungement from the temple rolls...?"

"You need to find a new jitte waver. I heard that Hambei Sayama was looking for people from the institute, and when I came to him with a made-up story, he bought it completely." Matsukichi laughed. "As did you! Did you check my connection to Chokichi? Go ahead, poke around. There's no beggar by the name of Matsukichi under his protection. Of course, he'd have told you there was—I paid him enough for that."

The man was obviously several steps ahead of Jinnai. The Conch and Taiko were good. He must have sprung into action as soon as Jinnai started looking into the refinery's finances for Kakita.

And now Jinnai was confused. His deduction that the empress was an automaton appeared to be correct, but how did these two fit into the story?

"Keian Higa visited the imperial palace many times to inspect the Sacred Vessel," said Kyuzo. "During that period, the reigning empress conceived her second child—potentially the

156

first girl born to the imperial line in many years. But, cruelly, the empress died in childbirth, and the gods soon reclaimed her newborn daughter as well. The imperial household was already reliant on the shogun not just for the funds to relocate the capital but for everything else. To keep him from insinuating himself further into imperial business, they formulated a plan: until a girl was born in the line of direct succession, they would replace the heir who had just died with an automaton—and make it the new empress."

Jinnai gasped.

"It was the Vessel, passed down within the imperial family since the Age of Myth, that made this plan possible. Keian was the first outsider permitted to inspect it, and the knowledge he gleaned let him create something thought to be impossible: an automaton indistinguishable from a human. You found the plans he drew up, in that book entitled *The Mechanism's Workings Are Obscure*."

The volume, as Jinnai had discovered in the library, contained elaborate diagrams of the Sacred Vessel—a human automaton. It explained that the Vessel had been locked up in an iron cabinet that stood in a cavern underneath the imperial tomb that had been closed off during the Age of Myth, and it detailed how the "empress" had been built in imitation.

The schematics included in the book began with an automaton in the form of an infant. This had been remade for key occasions so that it was always the expected age. Keian had secretly been entrusted with the work of research, maintenance, and reconstruction, which necessitated regular visits to the palace.

"The plan was to yield the throne to the first daughter born to the imperial family. But no heir was born for five years, then ten. Eventually, certain shogunate officials came to view this with suspicion."

"My patrons, the Conch and Taiko," said Matsukichi. "You know how Keian Higa's story ended. I don't think his aim was to protect the imperial secret. I think he just loved the imperial automaton he had made, like any father loves his daughter. He decided to topple the shogunate before she could be exposed, gathering ronin and building weapons the likes of which you've never seen. His plan was to strike simultaneously in Tempu and Kamigata, decapitate the shogunate by burning down Tempu Castle, and then have the automated empress order him to bring the remnants to heel."

But a traitor among Keian's secret army ended the plot before it could be set into action. That informant had ended up in the Muta domain. And Muta, after the incident at last year's cricket-fighting tournament, no longer existed.

"Keian's students were rounded up, leaving no one to repair or remake the empress. The imperial household claims that a grave illness has halted her growth, trapping her forever in her youthful form, and she no longer emerges from her quarters."

"I assume," said Jinnai hoarsely in the stifling atmosphere, "the fact that you haven't been hunted down by the palace despite what you know indicates that the Conch and Taiko are keeping this secret to themselves rather than sharing it with the shogun."

In other words, the Conch and Taiko were planning their own revolt against the shogunate.

They were probably plotting some kind of reform from

within that would let them retain their current position within the public service, rather than an armed coup like Keian had envisioned. They had swiped enough information to give them all the cards, but they were playing them close to their chest.

"Excellent deduction," said Matsukichi. "The Conch and Taiko sent someone to the Institute of Machinery to guide the situation. And that mole was..." He glanced to his side.

Jinnai followed his gaze. "Kyuzo Kugimiya?!" he exclaimed. He had expected to learn that Kyuzo had been one of Keian's students but not that he was an agent for the Conch and Taiko.

Kyuzo's eyes were cold and still, his expression utterly unchanging. "I had already made a name for myself in Tempu as a karakuri builder of some skill," he said. "You watched the show at Nakasu Kannon with Eve, I think? My designs, both of them. Early pieces."

"We wanted to know the secret of the Vessel," said Matsukichi, "so we recruited Kyuzo here and sent him to enroll in the institute. I'd have gone myself, but I don't know anything about chemistry or mechanics—I'd have been discovered right away."

Matsukichi held out his hand.

"I think it's time you handed over what you stole," he said. "I knew I could count on you to get it out of the refinery if I told you the title. Now I can get it to the Conch and Taiko before someone who actually understands it joins the refinery."

"And once I give it to you," said Jinnai, "you'll have no further use for me."

"Again, excellent deduction."

It was the perfect plan. Matsukichi hadn't been able to break into the refinery to steal the book himself—if he got caught, the

Conch and Taiko would immediately come under suspicion. Kyuzo, as refinery assistant, could have consulted or even borrowed the volume but not disposed of it, and his attentions might also signal to others that the book was of interest.

And so they had manipulated Jinnai, who had no connection to either of them, into bringing it right to them.

"You're not getting the book." Jinnai's hand found the hilt of his sword. "I'm going to take it to the authorities and clear my name."

"Not likely. The magistrate's office has no idea what the Conch and Taiko are plotting. They think they just sit around tooting on shells all day," Matsukichi said, miming the action.

Suddenly there was a slim dagger in his hand.

Jinnai popped the seal of his own sword.

"Don't you two know how to behave in someone else's house?" said Kyuzo, standing behind Matsukichi. But the other two already had their full concentration focused on each other's movements and did not reply.

A bead of sweat from Jinnai's forehead ran down his temple, then his jaw. Finally it dripped from his chin.

As it hit the floor, Jinnai broke the standoff, his hand moving a fraction before Matsukichi's followed suit.

Then came the boom of exploding gunpowder.

For a moment, Jinnai wasn't sure what had happened.

Matsukichi, already moving toward him, collapsed to the floor.

Kyuzo stood behind him with a short, oddly shaped pistol in his hand. White smoke still rose from the barrel.

"Vintage Keian Higa," he said. "I'd never tried firing it before.

160

Certainly does the job."

Matsukichi groaned, scrabbling at the floor in a growing pool of his own blood.

"Shot but still alive," said Kyuzo. "Just like a real lizard?"

"Kyuzo," snarled Matsukichi. "You..." He glared up at the other man, his face twisted with rage.

"What's happening here?" asked Jinnai, warily keeping the point of his sword toward Kyuzo.

"I'm finally free of this unsavory fellow," said Kyuzo coolly, "and I have your help to thank for it. Even from behind, I never found an opportunity to take him on. This was a once-in-a-lifetime chance." He glanced up at Jinnai and nodded. "Finish him."

After a moment's hesitation, Jinnai ran the blade through Matsukichi's throat. The man croaked like a frog and breathed his last.

Kyuzo crouched to confirm that Matsukichi's heart had stopped, then rose to his feet. "No time to waste," he said. "First we go to the master of the Conch and Taiko and arrange for him to clear you with the magistrate. You will be his new agent, replacing Matsukichi. Secrets are better shared with as few as possible, after all."

It appeared that Kyuzo had another plan, but Jinnai was in no position to object. Presumably the money matters that had attracted the attention of the master of accounts would be quietly forgotten in the confusion as well.

"I have no idea what's going on," Jinnai said.

"Weren't you listening earlier?" Kyuzo shook his head sorrowfully. "I was a simple karakuri maker when Matsukichi recruited me as a mole at the Institute of Machinery. I had neither the money nor the introductions to enroll on my own, so the proposal was just what I needed. At first, I thought only of stealing the technology and know-how of the great Keian Higa, but after a few years as his student, I had fallen under his sway. But Matsukichi was an intelligence agent. I knew that if I disappointed him my life would be forfeit, so I never revealed anything to Keian, even when I became one of his most trusted disciples."

Kyuzo's remorse was palpable.

"When I became involved in the construction of the imperial automaton, I started wishing I could see the Sacred Vessel for myself. But that wish was never granted. Keian's plot was revealed, and he was beheaded. The Conch and Taiko made sure that their mole was set free, and I found work at the refinery as an assistant. But I still regret letting Matsukichi talk me into infiltrating the institute. I should have lived out my days as just another karakuri maker."

Kyuzo spoke haltingly as he looked down at Matsukichi.

Some called Kyuzo Kugimiya a genius of automata. Others called him a demon. But Jinnai had not expected to discover this side of him.

When Kyuzo finally left the room, Eve came in directly.

"Eve," said Jinnai.

"Make your preparations. We have to visit the Conch and Taiko," she said.

And smiled.

VII

Jinnai stood before the hundred-prayer stone at Nakasu Kannon, waiting for the abacus to reach ninety-nine.

"Jinnai," Eve said, eyes widening just a fraction, when she returned to find him leaning against the pillar.

"I never did thank you properly," said Jinnai with a smile.

Without replying, Eve pushed the final tab on the abacus into place and turned to walk toward Ten-Span Bridge.

Jinnai fell into step beside her. "I'll be leaving Tempu soon," he said.

"I see."

Kihachi had delivered the news of his new assignment in a different province only yesterday.

Kyuzo had pulled a string here and there to have the magistrate's warrant canceled and Jinnai made the new spy for the Conch and Taiko.

Kyuzo's goals had been to eliminate Matsukichi and free himself from surveillance. Eve had recognized Jinnai as an intelligence agent from his first overtures, and it appeared that Kyuzo had been positioning him to replace Matsukichi all along.

Officially, his new assignment far from Tempu was a punishment from Kihachi, overseer of the Garden of August Repose, for having come under suspicion by the magistrate's office. In fact, he was being sent by the master of the Conch and Taiko to investigate the reclusive empress.

"Kyuzo feels bitter remorse for what he did," Eve said. "I am proof of that. He helped me escape from the institute before the shogunate ransacked it and continues to treat me as his daughter instead of surrendering me to them."

"So when you told me you weren't his real daughter..."

Eve smiled at him. "Are you wondering if I am Keian Higa's daughter instead?"

"Aren't you?"

"You are an intriguing man, Jinnai Tasaka," she said, stopping in the middle of the path. "So perceptive, and yet sometimes you overlook the most pertinent truths of all."

The stream of people on the road flowed around them as they stood on the path.

"I come here to pray that one day I might become human."

Jinnai doubted his ears at first, not comprehending. "No," he said. "Surely not."

"Foolish of me, I know. But we are free to wish as we will, are we not?"

Eve began to walk again.

"Does that mean you were created by Keian?" asked Jinnai.

This would make her a kind of sister to the imperial automaton.

"Kyuzo appears to think so."

"What does that mean?"

Eve stopped again at the very top of the arched bridge. She leaned over the railing and gazed into the river. The seabirds perched on the poles took to the air in a flurry of wings and flew off toward the gilded tiles of Kannon-do.

"Do you remember when we spoke about not being able to cross the same river twice?" she asked.

Jinnai nodded. He remembered that conversation well but had yet to understand what she had meant by it.

"Keian designed the imperial automaton based on the Sacred Vessel. He inspected and analyzed the Vessel for years, examining even the smallest detail and replacing parts one by one in the name of maintenance."

Jinnai joined Eve at the railing. A boat laden with fishing nets was slowly passing under the bridge.

"True artisans of automata—Keian was the same way—cannot abide letting the unknown slip from their grasp. If they can keep it close at hand, they do; if not, they strive at least to record it in writing."

Jinnai looked at Eve beside him as he struggled to grasp her import. Her profile bore the same melancholy expression as the one he had seen at the karakuri puppet show.

"Suppose you replaced every part of an automaton, component by component, and reassembled the parts you removed into a new automaton entirely. Which would be the real one?"

She turned her dark eyes to his, and a chill ran down his spine as he felt, just for a moment, as if he were looking at thousands of years of memories.

All the way back to the Age of Myth.

"What they call the Sacred Vessel sleeps even now in the imperial tomb," she said.

"But if I understand you correctly..."

"By inspecting my person down to the smallest detail, Kyuzo's mastery of automata came to rival even Keian's," she said with another smile. "He says that his dream is to inspect the Sacred Vessel for himself. Should that dream ever come true, I hope he is not disappointed."

With a parting nod, Eve began the descent to the other side of the bridge. Jinnai stood and watched her go, as if in shock.

In the far distance, the usual smoke billowed from the refinery chimneys.

RENEGADE GEPPETTO

I

"Now hear this: the day is come!"

When the court lady's voice rang out in the attendant's quarters, Kasuga sat up and rubbed her sleepy eyes.

Alongside the other ladies of the innermost sanctum—all girls her age—she briskly pulled on her uniform of a white habutai silk *marusode* over scarlet *hakama* trousers.

Once dressed, Kasuga left their quarters with the other girls, laughing quietly and commenting on the cold.

Even after pulling on her long *uchiki* as outerwear, Kasuga was still shivering. Pale crimson had only just begun to color the eastern sky, and her breath came in white clouds.

The attendant's quarters were in a triangular courtyard surrounded by a high stone fence. The palace had four other courtyards of the same shape, encompassing a larger pentagonal space at the middle to form a five-pointed star. This prevented anyone from moving between courtyards without passing the imperial tomb at the center.

In the imperial palace, "day" came only with the waking of the empress. At this signal, the rest of the residents began to stir as well.

In the past, the empress had woken at the same time every morning, with a regularity that was almost mechanical. Over the past year or so, however, her health had worsened, and "day" sometimes began before sunrise, forcing the attendants to hurry their morning chores, or she might not wake till the sun was high in the sky and everyone was anxious and impatient.

Kasuga heard a long, low tone. The palanquin bearers must have started the fires.

The palace compound contained a network of countless iron pipes. The pipes would freeze solid overnight, but when the wood-burning furnaces and the points of the star were lit in the morning, steam would pass through the pipes again, making them ring out musically as they thawed.

This system had been constructed by the refinery when the palace had been moved to this site thirty years ago, and it was used by the kitchen as well as for heating. They had been inspected many times to discover why they made their musical noises despite being jointed seamlessly, but no answer was forthcoming. It was simply one of the mysteries of life at the palace.

The corridor between the attendants' courtyard and the central pentagon was raised to keep their feet clear of impurity. Kasuga and her group opened a heavy door in the pentagon's thick raised-earth wall, revealing the tomb in the courtyard.

Of course, the imperial tomb itself was just a low mound perhaps twenty or thirty feet around. What was peculiar about it was the ominous heft of the cover that sealed it up.

A dome of thick iron covered the entire mound, and the exterior of the dome was crisscrossed by iron catwalks as if to hold it in place. The rust was scoured off once a year, but the surface of the blackly gleaming sphere had reddened in places all the same. Thin white steam rose from the iron, as if it were heated from below.

The overall impression was that the tomb had been hurriedly sealed up and then covered with several layers on top of that. There was not a hint of the elegance and splendor that characterized the rest of the palace.

In the dim early-morning light, beyond the shadows of the dome, Kasuga saw smoke pouring from the furnace chimneys. The whole palace should be awake by now, but she heard nothing except the pipes groaning like a wild beast.

When the palace had been moved there, the imperial tomb had already been in place. The moving procedure began with a ritual formula inscribed on a great turtle's plastron, which was then thrown into a fire. The cracks from the flames were interpreted by augurs to reveal where the palace should be moved, and the plastron last time had indicated that the most suitable location was the imperial tomb in which the Sacred Vessel rested.

Although the tomb thus stood at the center of the largest pentagonal courtyard and therefore the entire palace, few gave it much thought. Even to approach it too closely was forbidden, and Kasuga, like the others, had only seen it from afar when passing through one of the raised corridors.

The group made their way toward the empress's bedchamber.

Court ladies were only permitted as far as the outer rooms. An attendant led them through the hall to a door of cryptomeria wood with a dragon painted on it, which was the entrance to the empress's private quarters, known as the inner rooms.

Beyond the dragon door stood a gentlewoman. She led Kasuga and the others along a raised corridor to the inner rooms proper, where they dropped to their knees and crawled through the vestibule into the empress's private quarters.

This sequence was repeated every morning, and Kasuga never failed to find it tiresome.

There was a reason that their guide changed so frequently. Court ladies were barred even from the outer rooms; attendants were permitted in the outer rooms but no further; the inner rooms were restricted to gentlewomen and others who attended the empress directly, including Kasuga and the other ladies of the innermost sanctum.

How closely a person was permitted to approach the imperial person was strictly determined by birth and rank. The empress's most private rooms were off-limits to all but family members, those specifically selected for the position like Kasuga, and a handful of exceptions like nursemaids, physicians, and so on. Even those at the highest level of the palace bureaucracy, the most senior ladies-in-waiting and women of the chambers, did not have access.

On the other hand, among the attendants who served in the inner rooms, the ladies of the innermost sanctum were at the bottom of the hierarchy, lower even than the equerries. For that reason, even in the outer rooms they were barely viewed as human, and those who served in the inner rooms often ignored them completely.

It was customary for daughters of the lowest-ranking noble houses to work for a few years somewhere in the palace. A household that could place its daughter beyond the veil, in the innermost sanctum, could attain status equal to an archivist of the sixth rank.

Kasuga entered the bedchamber to find the empress still under the covers, lying on her back.

As usual, she was staring blankly into space.

The bed was surrounded by white damask curtains with a peony motif, but these had already been raised by the two ladies who had been stationed in the neighboring room overnight. Kasuga had nothing to do but wait for the empress to rouse herself.

The legs of the empress's sleepwear ended in something like socks to prevent her feet coming into direct contact with her bedding. Her slender arms were crossed lightly over her chest.

Her chestnut hair was slightly wavy and came down to her waist, and her eyes had the translucent hue of amber.

At her first sight of the empress, Kasuga had gasped. Although nearly thirty years old, she looked like a girl of fourteen or fifteen, no older than Kasuga herself.

It was said that grave illness had halted her physical development, and the ladies of the innermost sanctum believed this too. The conversations Kasuga overheard in their quarters expressed sincere pity for the empress's plight. Some of the more ingenuous girls even wept for her.

Those who served in the innermost sanctum were forbidden from addressing the empress on their own initiative. Not even greetings were permitted. Accordingly, for Kasuga to urge the empress to get up was completely out of the question. She could only wait silently until the empress did so of her own accord.

Kasuga stepped out of the innermost sanctum with two other girls to make the preparations for the empress's morning toilet. They tied their sleeves back with *tasuki* cords as they made their way to the bathing chamber elsewhere in the inner rooms.

The bathing room contained a tub of fragrant wood fed by warm water from the heated pipe system. The tub was already full to overflowing and was billowing steam.

Kasuga and the two other girls used a small wooden pail to fill a large washtub with hot water, then carried it back between the three of them. This was among the more physically taxing chores in the innermost sanctum, especially for young girls. What was more, the corridors here were entirely floored with tatami mats, meaning that not a drop could be spilled on them.

Returning to the bedchamber, they found the empress already sitting up. Another servant was helping her undress.

Her skin was smooth and white as porcelain, and the first swellings of her breasts were tipped with nipples like delicate pink sakura buds. She was hairless between her legs—probably naturally so, since Kasuga had never heard of anyone being called upon to help her shave.

The empress leaned over the washtub Kasuga and the others had brought and scooped handfuls of water up to her face.

When this was done, it was time for the four servants present to soak silk cloths in the hot water, wring them firmly, and then work together to scrub every inch of the empress's body. The empress stood naked and motionless, feet a shoulder span apart and both arms raised to a horizontal position, waiting for them to finish. She did not even twitch.

The girls helped the empress slip into a gown, neatly combed and coiffed her hair, and then applied her white powder and red lipstick. Next, the empress headed for "the eastern quarter"— the lavatory.

Kasuga had heard that the empress would extend her arm from behind the curtain for her physician to take her pulse while she was occupied there, but she had never seen it herself. Not even the ladies of the innermost sanctum accompanied the empress to the eastern quarter. It was Kasuga's understanding that a woman with the title *osashi* was charged with the specific duties of burning incense and wiping the imperial posterior once her business was done, but again, she had never met such an official. Perhaps due to the nature of their duties, they were separated from Kasuga and the other attendants intentionally.

Once the empress returned, it was time for breakfast, or "first repast" in the language of the palace.

"Now hear this: first repast has begun!"

Just like the announcement of the day's dawning, the cry passed from the gentlewomen to the attendants in the outer rooms, then to the court ladies and beyond, spreading voice by voice throughout the quiet palace that was by now enveloped in bright morning sunshine.

"Kasuga."

Startled at the voice, Kasuga looked around but saw no one.

Perhaps she had imagined it. She had certainly been nodding off.

Kasuga was sitting beside the empress's bed. The curtain was now lowered again, the bedchamber lit by a paper lantern, and Kasuga was waiting impatiently to hear the long, even breathing of sleep from within. She must have dozed off herself.

Like the dawning of the day and first repast, the empress's slumber had to be conveyed to the rest of the palace too. Alignment with the empress's movements was the fundamental law of the palace, so Kasuga's role here was an important one. If the empress did not fall asleep, most of her staff could not either, in case she decided to summon them.

Which meant that if Kasuga fell asleep and failed to alert the gentlewomen of the inner rooms, the entire palace would remain on standby all night without a minute's sleep.

Kasuga crawled forward quickly and listened to the sounds within the curtain around the imperial bed.

"Kasuga."

That voice.

She looked around again.

Why was she hearing a voice when there was no one in the room with her?

She got goose bumps at the thought before suddenly remembering that there *was* someone in the room with her.

The empress.

But Kasuga was dubious.

She had joined the women of the innermost sanctum two years ago, and in all that time she had never heard the empress speak.

To report the empress's sleeping and waking, two of the ladies of the inner sanctum stayed in the imperial quarters each night. One was there in case the empress woke in the night with business to assign, and she spread her bedding beside the empress's bed. The other slept in a neighboring room.

Tonight, Kasuga was the first of these two. There was no one she could turn to for confirmation of what she had heard.

Nor would it do for her to ask the empress if she had called her. She would just have to peer behind the bed curtains and check.

She slipped her fingers through where the curtains met and parted them an extremely modest inch or so.

Looking through the crack, she saw that the empress was awake and sitting up amid the blankets spread on the black lacquered dais that was her bed.

She was also looking back at Kasuga—and laughing, hand over her mouth for propriety's sake. Kasuga's attempts at stealth must have amused her.

Kasuga froze.

She froze, fingers still in the curtains, body hunched forward to peer through. She felt a flash of anxiety. Was she actually doing something extremely impolite?

"Kasuga. That is your name, we believe? We have been calling to you for some time without receiving an answer. Were you asleep?"

"F—forgive me, Your Majesty," said Kasuga, both mortified and astonished. Her voice came out as a squeak. Without getting off her knees, she sprang back at least two feet like a shrimp, then pressed her forehead to the floor.

"You are an amusing one," the empress said. "Go and tell the gentlewomen that we are asleep. I hope you will then indulge us in some light conversation."

Kasuga heard the empress chuckle whenever she wasn't speaking.

She left the bedchamber as instructed to announce that the august slumber had begun. It felt like a dream, a fantasy, but if the empress willed it she could only obey.

As the chain of voices began passing on the news into the distance, she returned to the dim chamber to find one of the bed curtains fully raised. Had the empress done this herself?

Beyond the curtains, she saw the empress in her sleepwear beckoning to Kasuga with a smile.

II

After Tempu's famed Thirteen Floors, the cluster of red-lantern establishments on the banks of the Ashikari River just outside Kamigata made a distinctly seedy impression.

Despite its relative proximity to the imperial palace, the scene put visitors in mind of the Sanzu River of myth, where unfortunate souls unable to cross over to the underworld were said to wander in limbo. Huts leaned together in rows, shingled roofs supported by posts sunk directly into the earth. A gaunt dog walked down the road through gritty clouds of dust.

But in an upstairs room at the best teahouse in the neighborhood, Jinnai Tasaka sat by a window sipping sake from a shallow cup and surveying the stone walls of the palace in the distance.

The chimneys at the palace's five outer points reminded him

of the refinery. Their white smoke drifted into the sky.

"Messengers from the shogun urging the empress to abdicate have been more frequent of late," said the man sitting opposite Jinnai.

"Who handles state affairs?"

"Prince Hiruhiko has performed that duty during the empress's long illness."

Jinnai nodded. Hiruhiko was the reigning empress's older brother. As a male child, he had no right to the throne himself, but his wife had recently given birth to a daughter.

His guest was a man who looked to be of the nobility but who was currently fidgeting before a tray of food and sake. Eager to call in the women, no doubt, but he would just have to wait until their conversation was over.

A senior attendant at the palace, the man had been cultivated by the Conch and Taiko as an informant, although whether he himself realized this was questionable.

Jinnai considered Hiruhiko's situation thoughtfully.

Imperial succession ran through the female line.

Officially, only those born of an empress were considered part of the imperial bloodline.

Hiruhiko's wife was a daughter of the shogun. Thirty years ago, the imperial household had borrowed most of the funds to move the palace from the shogunate, and when the period of mourning for the previous empress was over and the shogun had proposed a union between Prince Hiruhiko and the shogun's then five-year-old daughter Mari, the palace had been unable to refuse.

Hiruhiko and Mari had not been blessed with an heir for some years, but they were now the parents of an eagerly awaited daughter of at least partly imperial blood.

If the reigning empress abdicated, the throne would surely be inherited by Hiruhiko's daughter. As she was not yet old enough even to toddle on her own, Hiruhiko would act as her regent, continuing to control affairs of state as he presently did. When his daughter reached her majority and took up the responsibilities of her position, the absorption of the imperial household into the shogun's family would be complete.

A great reversal, with the shogun supreme above the empress at whose pleasure he technically served.

Hence the frequent messengers urging abdication.

There were rumors that the reigning empress's long illness might already have rendered her barren, though no one dared speculate publicly. In any case, every year she aged made the prospect of children less likely. Talk of marriage prospects had ceased, and her day-to-day affairs were left in the hands of a group of young girls known as "the ladies of the innermost sanctum." And it seemed doubtful that she would take one of the boys who did odd jobs around the palace as a concubine. In fact, rumor had it that at the age of almost thirty the empress was still a virgin.

"I want to speak to someone close to the top," said Jinnai, raising his cup to his lips. By "top," of course he meant the empress.

"Close?"

"A servant. Someone who attends to her everyday needs."

The senior attendant looked pained.

The reigning empress's mother had died in childbirth. For a

time there had been rumors that the child had been stillborn also, but these had eventually been dispelled.

Her father had been one of the palace boys—an entirely different sort of man from Prince Hiruhiko. After the empress had ascended to the throne, he had been promoted to chief of servants but had later succumbed to a fatal illness of unknown cause.

"That I cannot do," said the senior attendant finally.

His reluctance caught Jinnai by surprise. The man was tougher than he had expected. Bottling up his irritation, Jinnai said, "If it's a question of money..."

The man shook his head. Apparently this was not the issue. "The only ones who see Her Majesty directly are the ladies of the innermost sanctum," he said. "Girls, none yet in their fifteenth year. Money is unlikely to prove much inducement to them."

His speech was beginning to slur from drink, but on this matter he was quite firm.

"I see," said Jinnai with a nod. The palace must keep the number of people in direct contact with the empress as low as possible.

In Tempu, the only people who knew that the empress was an automaton outside the Conch and Taiko were Jinnai himself and Kyuzo Kugimiya. It was the secret among secrets, shared only with a select few even among the imperial household. Prince Hiruhiko must know, but the man across the table from Jinnai right now clearly did not.

"Also," he continued, "once a girl becomes a lady of the innermost sanctum, she may not set foot outside the palace again until the conclusion of her service. I could not bring one to meet you even if she were willing."

"Are there any whose service is about to conclude, then?"

"Well..."

Sake had loosened the man's tongue easily, but he clammed up now. Not a difficult man to understand, Jinnai thought, reaching for the small porcelain bottle and pouring him another cup.

"The other day, one of the ladies of the innermost sanctum... was careless. She will be leaving the palace soon."

"'Careless'? What does that mean?"

"I am not privy to the details."

"Is there a lot of carelessness at the palace?"

"Rarely. The ladies of the innermost sanctum serve terms of a few years. Once they turn fifteen, they are either made court ladies or sent back to their homes."

"I gather that neither of those fates await those who are careless?" said Jinnai, pursuing the man relentlessly.

"In confidence..." The man looked around nervously. His aversion must have been to speaking the words themselves aloud, because the chances of anyone eavesdropping on their conversation were low.

"They're going to kill her?" Jinnai said, when the man continued to have trouble finding the words.

A nod.

Jinnai's expression remained impassive as things clicked into place in his mind.

The girl must have discovered the truth.

She knew that the empress was an automaton.

Reducing the empress's personal staff to an absolute minimum would not be enough to ensure that the secret remained hidden. Keeping each attendant's term of service short and forbidding them to leave the palace for the duration was clearly another part of the strategy.

Even so, every so often someone in close contact with the empress would see through the facade. It appeared that those unfortunate souls were condemned to death.

"Tell me more," Jinnai said.

He put a hint of iron into his voice, knowing that the man would cringe before it.

If all those who learned the empress's secret were executed for "carelessness," questioning those who had served as attendants in their youth would be pointless. Even those who did know the truth would never speak it, knowing that their circumspection was what had allowed them to finish their term of service unharmed.

Jinnai made his decision. He would have to abduct this girl marked for death and interrogate her instead. This would give him proof that the empress was alive as well as more information about her current state.

"Are executions performed at the palace?"

"Bloodshed on the palace grounds is generally frowned upon."

So she would be taken elsewhere. Good. Breaking into the palace and kidnaping someone from the innermost sanctum would have been a tall order even for Jinnai.

"The girl herself doesn't know that she's going to her death, does she?"

The man shook his head. This was logical. They didn't want

the girl to make a break for it once they were outside the palace walls.

"All right. Send word to me when the day is decided. What's the girl's name?"

"Kasuga."

Jinnai nodded and clapped his hands. Several ladies of pleasure who had been waiting outside the room came in.

The palace attendant's grim expression was gone in an instant.

Jinnai remained entirely sober as he watched the man settle in for an evening of debauchery.

If this was the man who managed the attendants of the palace's outer rooms, then he had a fairly good idea of the class of person who supported the imperial household.

A man who spoke secrets so freely would speak of Jinnai too.

Once this was all over, Jinnai would have to quietly eliminate him.

A woman sat down beside Jinnai, and he slipped his hand into the front fold of her kimono, groping without much enthusiasm for her breast.

III

"Closer."

The empress beckoned from within the bed-curtains.

Kasuga crawled numbly toward the lacquered dais.

"Closer still," said the empress.

Kasuga hesitated. Was she to climb onto the bed itself? She sensed an almost supernatural power in the ring of the empress's words, the pale crimson of her parted lips.

And then, with a start, she woke.

She had been riding in the palanquin for almost an hour. The boredom and the swaying must have lulled her into a fitful sleep.

We know what you are, Kasuga...

She recalled the words the empress had spoken that night.

Yes. Her Majesty knew all, saw all.

Kasuga had watched as the empress loosened the obi of vermillion crepe around her waist and removed her sleepwear of white silk with its socked feet.

She had seen the empress's skin many times before but still gasped at how white and sharp it was in the paper lantern's bleary light.

"Touch us."

The empress gripped Kasuga's wrist with a surprisingly cold hand.

The ladies of the innermost sanctum were strictly forbidden from allowing their skin to come into contact with the empress's, even when attending her at her bath, combing her hair, or helping her dress. Another measure to protect her purity from pollution, just like the socks of her sleepwear.

But now, with no regard for this injunction, the empress brought Kasuga's hand to her chest.

The empress's ribs were just visible through her skin. Just over her sternum, between the slight swellings of her breasts, Kasuga's hand made contact.

Something that was plainly not a heart beat out a rhythm inside.

Kasuga raised her head and looked at the empress.

In her amber eyes she saw her own reflection.

The empress placed her hands on Kasuga's cheeks and drew her nearer, hugging the girl's head to her bosom.

With a sob, Kasuga pressed her ear to the empress's chest.

Through the cold skin she heard the rhythm from before, clearer and louder than when it had come to her through touch alone.

Kasuga closed her eyes.

The faint metallic tick of a balance wheel swinging back and forth and striking a pendulum.

Gears large and small, teeth precisely interlocked, whirring as the clockwork drove them.

In the darkness behind her closed eyes, Kasuga saw the mechanisms packed into the empress's body spread out before her and felt peace and comfort.

So the empress truly is—

But before she could finish the thought, the empress spoke.

"You understand now, we think, that we are not human." She spoke of herself, *pluralis maiestatis*, as an empress must.

Kasuga opened her eyes. The empress's face was only a breath away.

"Our person has been deprived of maintenance for many years. Since our father, Keian Higa, departed from this world."

Kasuga knew the name. A conspirator against the shogun who had been caught and executed, he was also the greatest karakuri designer of his time.

"Before long, we believe that our mechanisms will cease to operate."

"No," Kasuga said, eyes welling with tears. The empress ran her fingers through Kasuga's black hair, stroking her head.

"If that should come to pass, will you protect us?"

Kasuga nodded. She had no idea how to make good on the promise, but she nodded.

"We thank you."

The empress touched her lips lightly to the back of Kasuga's neck.

And not long after that, there arrived a morning when the empress's day failed to dawn.

When the procession with the palanquin at its center emerged from the palace, it was the Hour of the Rat. The dead of night.

Ten or more torches bobbed in the night like ghost lights, illuminating the bridge as the group crossed the moat. They reached the highway and headed west, giving the distinct impression that they hoped not to be seen.

The date and time both matched what his informant had told him.

Jinnai, dressed in his black shinobi outfit to better melt into the darkness, howled like a wild dog to signal to Chokichi Yaguruma's men lying in wait nearby.

They were street toughs, unlikely to show much subtlety when they sprang into action. But Jinnai usually worked alone. When he needed backup, he could not be too choosy. And he had an existing connection to Chokichi since the business in Tempu not long ago.

So, after explaining the situation to the master of the Conch and Taiko, he had paid Chokichi a hefty sum to procure the corpse of a girl of fourteen or fifteen from the execution grounds and send it to Kamigata, along with a few men to assist him.

The plan was the height of simplicity. Chokichi's men, pretending to be highwaymen, would overwhelm the procession. The roads were dangerous around the palace, and

Chokichi's thugs were not so different from actual highwaymen in any case. The attack itself should not seem unusual.

Next, Jinnai would kill everyone who had emerged from the palace except for Kasuga, whom he would abduct, leaving the corpse in her place.

She was being carried to her death to begin with, so if she appeared to have been murdered along with the others, the outcry should be minimal. The entire incident might be hushed up.

Compared to the sort of work the shogun's intelligence service was capable of, this would be a simple operation. But since the people enacting it were common criminals rather than trained agents, Jinnai felt a degree of unease.

Following the procession soundlessly from a safe distance, Jinnai counted the torches. It would not do to overlook anyone during his slaughter.

Eventually they came to a crossroads with good visibility from all sides. Just as planned, the torches at the front of the procession began to gutter and shake.

Chokichi's men fell upon the group without even offering parley.

Drawing the short, straight shinobi sword at his waist, Jinnai closed the distance rapidly.

Although the procession's guards had been armed, Chokichi's men were cutting them down before they could even draw their swords from the magnificent scabbards that hung from their belts on embroidered cords. Jinnai saw one trying to scramble away on all fours without drawing his sword at all.

So much for palace security. Chokichi's men could probably handle this one on their own.

And then a figure leapt out of the palanquin itself, and the head of one of Chokichi's men went flying toward the moon.

What?

Jinnai reversed course at once, diving diagonally backward to take cover behind a row of half a dozen roadside statues—a sixfold Jizo, protector of children and travelers.

Chokichi's men bellowed with anger, and the shadowy figure ran between them with simian agility.

Another head flew through the air.

The figure did not seem to have a sword drawn. What it was using for a weapon was unclear, but it did not move like a warrior. A shinobi, then, or something of that nature.

Had this been a setup?

Jinnai considered the possibility for a split second.

If so, either his informant had betrayed him or their plan had leaked from somewhere else.

As Jinnai's mind raced, the shadowy figure continued to eliminate Chokichi's men with methodical precision. Soon there was no one else alive and moving at the crossroads, which had become a charnel house strewn with the corpses of the palanquin guards and Chokichi's men.

Jinnai had heard rumors that the imperial household had maintained a shinobi tradition of its own since ancient times. Could that be what he was seeing?

After some deliberation, he decided to confront the figure. The plan could not be aborted in any case.

He detached the empty scabbard from his waist and threw it into a stand of trees across the intersection.

The shadowy figure looked up from checking the pulses of its victims and stared in the direction the sound had come from. Jinnai remained absolutely motionless, waiting to see what the figure would do.

With careful tread, the figure began walking toward the stand of trees.

His ruse had worked.

But when Jinnai rose to hurl a throwing spike at the figure's back, it spun as if it had been waiting, sweeping its arm in a throwing gesture.

Jinnai leapt backward and flattened himself to the ground just in time. He saw a flash of reflected moonlight, and the heads of the six Jizo statues he had been hiding behind thudded to the ground one by one.

Wire.

The figure was using a thin wire with a honed edge and weights at the end. Wrapped around a neck and pulled tight, it could lop off the head like cutting through tofu.

Jinnai had never faced an opponent with this kind of trick up its sleeve before.

Realizing that he would be killed if he stayed in one place too long, he sprang up and streaked diagonally across the intersection.

The figure ran after him.

Turning back, Jinnai crouched deeply, then leapt at his pursuer, flying so low that he almost scraped the ground.

As the wire sliced the wind above his head, Jinnai slashed at the figure's shins with his sword but only succeeded in nicking its distinctive *tattsuke-bakama* trousers, loose around the thigh but close-fitting from the knee down.

But now he was within striking distance.

He doubted the figure's wire tricks were effective at such close range.

Propelling himself up from the ground, Jinnai headbutted the figure's chin from below.

The figure grunted.

But it was Jinnai who was shocked.

The figure's voice was unmistakably female.

Seizing her by the front fold of her clothing as she staggered back, Jinnai used his full strength to swing them both around and throw her over his hip onto the ground. Without pausing for breath, he straddled and immobilized her. He pressed his elbow to her throat and kept it there until her struggling subsided.

Jinnai rose unsteadily to his feet and surveyed the carnage.

The torches dropped by the palace guards as they fell were still burning here and there on the ground.

Jinnai picked one up and used it to illuminate the palanquin, which sat alone and forgotten at the center of the intersection.

It was a sturdy and well-made vehicle. Its black lacquer finish was perhaps for stealth.

The woman who had killed Chokichi's men had emerged from the palanquin. If this procession had been a decoy, the palanquin was probably empty now, but he had to check.

Its doors still hung open.

Jinnai crouched to peer inside.

Inside, a girl shrank against the far corner in fear.

"Are you Kasuga?" He whispered so that his voice would not carry.

He brought the torch closer to see the girl's face. She gave the faintest of nods, terror in her eyes.

So the other woman had been riding with her in the palanquin. To make sure she did not escape?

His informant had told him nothing of Kasuga's appearance, but she was more slightly built than he had expected.

"Take off your clothes," he said, his tone making it clear that it was an order.

The corpse that Chokichi had procured for him was hidden in a barn not far from the intersection. Its face had already been rendered unrecognizable and its hair burned off. All that remained was to dress it in the girl's clothes to make it seem that she had died.

But, perhaps misunderstanding Jinnai's intentions, the girl in the palanquin shook her head, opening and closing her mouth without quite managing to speak.

Irritated, Jinnai threw the torch to one side, reached into the palanquin to seize the girl's ankles, and dragged her out in one swift motion.

She screamed and struggled, using all four limbs in an attempt to push him away. He slapped her face two or three times to silence her, then grabbed the obi at her waist and tore her clothes off.

The girl's unblemished white skin seemed to glow in the moonlit dark.

Now stripped to her underwear, the girl hurriedly concealed her breasts with her arms. Jinnai pulled off his own black shirt and pulled it over her head, then hoisted her over one shoulder and headed for the storehouse where the corpse was hidden.

Perhaps too petrified by now, the girl did not resist or scream as he bound her securely to a pillar and set off, again carrying the corpse, for the intersection.

He stuffed the body into the palanquin and then used another torch to set the wooden litter ablaze.

Turning his back on the flames, he returned to the barn, loosened the rough ropes binding the girl to the pillar, and gave her a kosode and obi in drab colors.

It would be dangerous to hide her too close to the palace, or anywhere people might recognize her. They would have to make the journey of a few days back to Tempu and then put into action the second phase of the plan, which Chokichi should be preparing for at that moment—to stash her in the Thirteen Floors. Her interrogation and the like could be carried out there. The master of the Conch and Taiko could even visit her in person if necessary.

Once his preparations for the journey were complete, Jinnai looked up and saw that the girl had put her sleeves through the kosode but had not tied the obi around herself. She looked at him helplessly, holding it in her hands.

"What's the matter?" he asked.

"I do not know how to tie it," she said.

"What?" His voice was louder than he had intended.

Everyone who served at the palace, right down to the lowliest servant, was a scion of some noble family or other. Jinnai had heard that their daily clothing was still the same as it had been since ancient times, but to someone of his upbringing, not even being able to tie an obi was unthinkable.

"Give it here," he said.

He had her raise her arms so that he could align the lapels

of her kosode, then reached around her waist to wrap the obi around her and tie it in place. He felt like her manservant. She looked used to the treatment. It made for a strange scene.

"What about trousers?" the girl asked, trying to pull down the hem of the kosode.

"There aren't any," Jinnai said shortly.

The women of the palace must still wear those vermillion hakama of old. If she was of noble birth, she might never have even seen the way the women of Tempu dressed today, with no hakama over their kosode.

Then he got down to business.

"I hear that you were expelled from the innermost sanctum for carelessness," Jinnai said. "Can you think of anything specific?"

The girl, who had been fidgeting with her knees together in embarrassment, sent a sharp glare his way.

"Specific?"

"For example, accidentally learning something the empress wanted kept secret. That sort of thing," Jinnai said with careful vagueness. If the girl didn't tell him what she knew in her own words, the exercise was pointless.

She didn't stop glaring at him, but she did seem to be thinking. Probably still trying to decide who he was and why he had abducted her.

"They were going to kill you," he said, holding her gaze. "Several other women who seemed to be former ladies of the innermost sanctum have met with the same end in the past. It's hard to believe that the palace would go so far to punish simple mistakes."

The girl was silent. He sensed she was hiding something.

"Fine. I'll have you in the mood to talk soon enough."

Alarm filled the girl's eyes at this ominous prediction. "Who *are* you?" she asked.

"I can't tell you that. But if you tell me the truth, we can offer you protection. I'd rather not make this unpleasant for either of us."

There was no room for sentiment in intelligence work, but even Jinnai was not enthusiastic about the prospect of torturing a mere girl.

"It'll take a few days to reach Tempu," he said. "Think it over on the way. I will say this—your life here is over. Returning to the palace or your family home is not an option."

The girl's eyes were already widening. "We're going to Tempu?" she said.

IV

"So. Tell me about this Kasuga."

"Surprisingly docile. Does as we tell her, without complaint," Jinnai said, refilling the cup of Lord Haga, governor of Hanyu, master of the Conch and Taiko. "As for the matter we discussed, however..."

Haga nodded. His face was flat and square, like a crab. He had beady eyes that tended to cross and a bulbous black mole at the center of his forehead like the third eye on the Great Buddha. To strangers he might have looked harmless, even lovable.

"We must seize this opportunity to stop an abdication," he said now. "If the shogunate absorbs the imperial family before we lay the groundwork, we'll be left with no room to maneuver. Where's Kyuzo, by the way?" He glanced sideways at a tray of refreshments that was still untouched, its sake cup inverted.

Kyuzo Kugimiya had been summoned to their meeting too, but an hour after the appointed time he had yet to show himself. For a mere tinkerer of automata to keep the master of the Conch and Taiko waiting was unheard of, but Kyuzo had little interest in protocol. Like Jinnai, he was an agent of sorts for the Conch and Taiko, but theirs was not a relationship built on trust between master and servant. Perhaps even drinking together was a distasteful idea to him.

Jinnai had been planning to call in the entertainment after Kyuzo arrived, but with Haga's mood darkening he was left with no choice but to move things along.

Haga's favorite courtesan entered the room with her entourage of trainees. She greeted her two guests effusively. The bowed strains of a *tiqin* filled the air, but Haga and Jinnai were not watching the dancer and her fan and hand cloth. They were looking at the youngest trainee, who sat at the very end of the line.

It was the girl Jinnai had abducted from the palanquin.

She may not have been accustomed to kneeling; in any case, she kept shifting with obvious discomfort. Once she noticed Jinnai in the room, she began stealing furtive glances his way.

She cleaned up surprisingly well with a change of wardrobe. Her chestnut hair had been cut in the style prescribed for the youngest trainees, the *kamuro*, and had apparently been straightened through careful brushing. In her white face powder and dab of red lipstick, she made a charming impression.

Jinnai had entrusted her to Haga's favorite courtesan after bringing her to Tempu. Not directly, of course; Chokichi had provided a middleman who claimed to have gotten her from a trafficker.

A kamuro in the Thirteen Floors was never alone. From the senior lady of pleasure she served to the other trainees, there was always someone nearby. Overseers and other staff also kept close watch on their charges.

Not even the magistrates could just barge into the Thirteen Floors whenever they pleased, and no one kept secrets better than the courtesans on its highest floors, where secret negotiations and exchanges were common. Having placed the girl here as a kamuro with hints of an awkward situation, they could rest assured that she would be safe.

The Thirteen Floors was the natural home of misfits and outcasts. Even if the girl spoke of her service at the palace, no one would take her seriously.

It was the ideal place to hide a girl you had kidnaped from the imperial palace.

When Kyuzo arrived and the revelries ended, they would have to find some excuse to call the girl into another room alone, Jinnai thought.

And then the Thirteen Floors shook with a tremendous explosion.

The women in the room screamed. The music ended abruptly.

Jinnai sprang to his feet, slid aside a black-framed paper screen, and stepped onto the gallery that opened to the outside. Leaning over the railing, he saw black smoke rising from under the tiled eaves of the floor below.

He quickly reentered the room to find that the guards Haga had stationed outside its door had already burst in to protect him. Men working for the Thirteen Floors were trying to get both visitors and employees out of the room.

"What is this?" demanded Haga, noticeably paler than before.

"An explosion on the floor below, it seems," said Jinnai. "You must get out quickly. I..."

"You what?"

Then the master of the Conch and Taiko noticed what Jinnai just had.

The girl was gone.

Haga gave Jinnai a look that said, *Go!*

Perhaps she had just been ushered to safety already by the men of the Thirteen Floors. But Jinnai found it difficult to imagine them putting a kamuro ahead of customers and senior courtesans.

He had a bad feeling about this.

What if the explosion had been engineered so that the girl could be stolen back?

Damage to the Thirteen Floors from suspicious fires was not unheard of, but the use of gunpowder was unthinkable.

The upper floors of the building were frequented by shogunate officials and emissaries from the provincial domains. The lower floors were where the masters of Tempu's underworld of thugs, gamblers, and criminals gathered. Disturbing the peace at the Thirteen Floors attracted attention from both high and low places, and that meant trouble. This was why even the magistrates had to exercise circumspection. Arson and bombings were utterly beyond the pale.

Whoever had done this either did not know these things or knew them and did not care. It must be someone with no connection to the Thirteen Floors at all.

The imperial household? But Tempu was a long way from Kamigata. How could they have traced the girl to here?

Jinnai ran into the inner corridor. The flames had yet to reach there, but the entire floor had descended into panic.

There were two wide staircases, but one of them billowed with the same black smoke he had seen outside. The other was crowded far beyond capacity with people who shoved and shouted at each other in their desperation to escape.

Jinnai dove into a room across the corridor from the one he and Haga had been in. He crossed the tatami mats in an instant, dodging tableware and sake bottles, and kicked down the paper screen on the far side to get to the gallery.

The fire had not reached this side of the building yet.

He vaulted the railing. Landing on the eaves of the floor below, he let himself slide down the steep tiles until he reached the edge. He caught hold of the gutter and used his momentum to change direction and hurl himself into the gallery directly below the one he had just been in.

Noticing that black smoke already filled the room behind it, he raced around the gallery, which ringed the floor, to get back to the original side of the building, where the explosion had gone off.

There.

He saw the girl. She was hoisted over the shoulder of someone who must have leapt over the gallery railing just moments earlier and was now heading for the canal far below. A figure in indigo work clothes.

The figure, he realized in a flash of intuition, that he had encountered at the crossroads near the palace.

In all the confusion of that night, he had forgotten to make sure that she had actually died. Sloppy.

She appeared to notice Jinnai as well, but ignored him and ran toward the canal.

He had to stop her. He pulled a throwing spike from the front fold of his kosode and let it fly.

But it only struck one of the lower railings, and the figure in indigo vaulted the bannister, still carrying the girl.

Another blast—Jinnai instinctively dove out of the path of the heat. A fireball erupted from within the building and blew out the paper screens along the outer corridor.

Wire glittered in the air, zipping by Jinnai, and wrapped itself around the railing. He peered over the edge.

The figure had used it to control her fall. All he saw on the surface of the canal more then twenty feet below was a remnant white splash.

He watched as the torn paper screens tumbled down toward the canal like great burning leaves.

V

"Sounds like *ukami* work."

In the inner courtyard of Tempu Castle, Kihachi Umekawa was wrapping a red pine in straw for the winter.

"Ukami?" repeated Jinnai.

"The empress's shinobi."

Jinnai held the mat of straw against the pine's trunk while Kihachi bound it in place with rough rope. Both were dressed in the same work clothes as any other gardener.

It had been several days since the disturbance at the Thirteen Floors. The flames had ultimately been contained to the floor they'd broken out on, and Jinnai had escaped unharmed.

The shogunate was not inclined to let the matter rest, however. No one had died in the blaze, but several rooms on the higher floors had been in use by high officials when the bomb had gone off.

Chokichi Yaguruma's men were also searching grimly for the parties responsible.

And now Jinnai had been summoned to this courtyard of white gravel at Tempu Castle to help wrap the trees in the Garden of August Repose for the winter. The request had come directly from Kihachi himself, head gardener and secret chief of the shogun's intelligence service.

This was unusual.

The shogun's spies sometimes visited Tempu Castle even when not on patrol duty if they wanted to consult with Kihachi on something, but this was the first time Kihachi had called one of them in.

He must have heard about Jinnai's involvement with the incident at the Thirteen Floors from somewhere. Chokichi's people, most likely.

Kihachi ordered Jinnai to tidy up around the pine, now snugly protected from the cold, and began spreading a sheet under the next tree, humming as he worked.

This was just like any other visit with Kihachi. Why had he been called here?

Jinnai knew that Kihachi was a wily conversationalist. People who came to question him ended up running off their mouths about all sorts of things. Jinnai very carefully sought only the information he needed from him, to keep the older man from rummaging through his secrets.

"The imperial household is a darker place than you think, Jinnai," said Kihachi. He nodded with satisfaction at the spread-out sheet and began wrapping the next mat of straw around the tree. "You need to look closely into what Kyuzo

Kugimiya is doing, and where."

After that, the conversation stayed on safer topics: the walnut cakes at the teahouses along the Okawa that the whole city was talking about, the new shows at Nakasu Kannon, the question of when exactly to burn the straw mats in spring. Then the work was done, and Jinnai left the castle.

He was almost disappointed. He had expected Kihachi to interrogate him on his assignments and what the master of the Conch and Taiko was planning. Why else go to the trouble of summoning him to the castle?

Since Kihachi's summons could not be ignored, Jinnai had secreted numerous weapons about his person, even bringing poison in case he had to end his own life. But none of it had been necessary.

So what was going on?

Try as he might, he could not figure it out.

He certainly didn't need Kihachi to tell him to investigate Kyuzo. Jinnai had checked the Kugimiya residence countless times since his failure to appear at the Thirteen Floors, but behind its high earthen walls both main house and workshop seemed utterly deserted.

Was it possible that Kyuzo and Eve had been kidnaped?

He know nothing of the ukami that Kihachi had mentioned, including the scale and scope of their organization. He had only come into contact with them twice.

Mulling the problem over, he made his way to Ganjin Canal. The canal flophouses were where he went to ground when temporarily back in Tempu.

He smelled the stagnant, polluted canal long before he saw

it. The narrow pathway along the canal bank was dotted with people sleeping, wrapped in filthy mats, unable to afford even a flophouse room. There was also the occasional drunkard, wandering around almost naked and growling in a too-loud voice about obscure grievances.

"Hey, Tasaka!"

The voice came from behind him, but he was not surprised. Someone had been following him for a while now. He stopped and turned to see who it was.

A small group of thugs glared back at him. Their heads were stubbly, and their beards were unkempt. Their clothes hung loose and sloppy. None of them wore shoes, but some had daggers at their belts and made sure Jinnai knew it.

Their poor attempt at creeping up on him had led him to assume they were just muggers or street toughs, but if they knew his name that changed the situation.

Jinnai sensed several other men emerging behind him, in the direction he had originally been walking. Accomplices who had been waiting in a convenient side alley, no doubt.

"That mess on the Thirteen Floors was a big embarrassment for us," said one of the men. "The boss wants a word with you."

Jinnai tutted to himself. First Kihachi, and now Chokichi?

This was what you got for making trouble on the Floors. Everyone had a bone to pick with you.

It was obvious what Chokichi wanted to talk about. He and Jinnai had remained in contact since the girl's abduction. If the magistrate's attentions turned to Jinnai, warrants for Chokichi and his men wouldn't be far behind. Jinnai could understand the man's agitation.

"Maybe another time," Jinnai said. "I'm trying to pin down whoever started the fire myself."

"All I know is the boss told us to bring you in," said the man.

Talking did not seem likely to work.

And, of course, Jinnai had no intention of following these clowns anywhere.

He doubted Chokichi had much more regard for them than he did, which meant cutting them down here wouldn't necessarily end his relationship with Chokichi as long as he made amends once everything was resolved.

The problem was there were too many of them. Even for Jinnai, ten against one were long odds. He decided to take down two or three quickly and run for it while the rest were still in shock.

When he shifted the sword on his hip, Chokichi's men tensed.

When he popped the scabbard with his left thumb, one of the jumpier men in the group charged him with a dagger.

Jinnai neatly sidestepped the blade, then turned to bring his sword down across the man's back as he stumbled past.

A scream echoed across Ganjin Canal.

Still gripping his sword, Jinnai ran forward.

The man in his direct path fumbled for his dagger, but before he could draw it Jinnai kicked off the ground and soared through the air to plant his foot directly on the man's chest, kicking him squarely into the filthy waters of the canal.

His escape route now open, Jinnai kept running and didn't look back.

Hurdling over drunks passed out in the gutter, ignoring the jeers of people watching from under the eaves along the path, Jinnai ran.

Chokichi's men gave pursuit, but their angry cries gradually receded as he got farther ahead of them. When he reached the end of the canal, he paused and looked back. Only a handful of men were still in sight, and they were exhausted, crouching where they were or slumped in doorways gasping for breath. Another was leaning over the edge of the canal and vomiting into it noisily. Running was hard on some people. Jinnai, on the other hand, was not even out of breath.

He could have gone back and finished them off in no time at all, but they looked so ridiculous to him that he just shook the blood off his sword and put it back in its scabbard.

He had something new to worry about.

A boat on the canal had been following him for the entire duration of his footrace with Chokichi's men. He had mistaken it for one of the many tiny covered boats with women aboard selling their affections, but on closer inspection he realized he was wrong.

As he watched, the boat's prow turned toward the edge of the canal.

More trouble? Jinnai's guard went back up. But then he heard a voice he recognized.

"Jin! Jin!"

Squinting, he saw a woman in a red kosode, sleeves tied back for practical work and hair wrapped up in a hand cloth, rowing furiously.

"Eve?!"

"So Kyuzo is still in hiding too?"

"Yes. He said something about important business to take care of."

The two of them were in the bathhouse's steam-filled washing area. Eve's sleeves were still held back with cords, and her kosode hem was rolled up above her knees. Once she finished scrubbing Jinnai's back with the bag of rice bran, she reached for a basin of hot water and dumped it cheerfully over his head.

A boy watching from nearby laughed. Jinnai rubbed his face with his palms and smiled ruefully.

"Do me next!" came a voice from elsewhere in the washing area.

Jinnai turned and saw a heavyset woman somewhere north of thirty years of age beckoning.

"O-Tomi! Don't overwork our Eve!" said the woman in the red high chair, who seemed to be in charge there.

Leaving Jinnai to fend for himself, Eve went to scrub the other woman's back. Jinnai found something peculiar in the sight. The melancholy air about her when doing her hundred prayers at Nakasu Kannon was nowhere to be seen. Instead, she was cheerful and bright—an entirely different person. She clearly enjoyed the work.

Jinnai stooped to pass through the low door to the men's bath and was pleased to find it unoccupied.

Easing himself into the steaming water right up to his shoulders, he finally felt human again.

You're being followed. It was the first thing Eve had told him back at the canal.

She didn't mean Chokichi's thugs, of course. She was talking about men who worked for Kihachi. The elite of the intelligence service's elite.

It seemed that Jinnai still had his freedom only because they wanted to see what he would do with it.

They must have followed him from the castle, watching to see where he went and whom he talked to. Perhaps they believed he was in contact with Kyuzo.

Knowing that Jinnai was moving from one flophouse to the next by Ganjin Canal, Eve had borrowed the bathhouse's old boat, the one that had once gone all the way to the Thirteen Floors, and launched it on the canal to wait for him.

Not even the shogun's spies could maintain their surveillance once he was aboard. No doubt they were currently grinding their teeth in frustration over his escape.

Jinnai emerged from the bath, slipped on a thin yukata, and ascended the narrow stairway into the changing area.

The room upstairs had a low ceiling, six feet at most, and Jinnai had to hunch his shoulders to cross the room. He was just oiling his hair when Eve appeared at the head of the stairs.

"I have to say," he said with a wry smile, "I didn't expect to find you lying low in a bathhouse."

"I am as loyal to Chitose as I would be to my mother," Eve said, removing the cords that held back her kosode's sleeves. Then she looked down, hands on her cheeks. "She even asked me to take over the high chair if Tentoku ever returns."

Was she blushing? A trick of the light, or the result of workings

Kyuzo had installed?

"Who's Tentoku?" he asked.

Eve's eyes went wide. "You don't *know*? Geiemon Tentoku, the wrestler! He used to work here too. He's dropped out of the public eye of late, for certain reasons. I first met Chitose when I came here to tell her that he was all right."

Jinnai shrugged. "Fine," he said. "Did you have anything else you came up here to tell me?"

They were the only two in the room, which was less busy during the day.

"Yes," Eve said, sitting up straighter. "In fact, I have something I want to ask you. You must not tell anyone—not even Kyuzo."

A secret even from Kyuzo? That was out of character. Whatever it was must be big.

"I think that Kihachi's men are watching his residence."

Jinnai nodded. If they were following him, they would hardly leave Kyuzo's house unguarded.

"After Kyuzo saved your life, he told me to hide here until the heat died down. But..."

"But?"

"If we leave the Kugimiya residence empty too long, someone might burn it down. I cannot tell you how much this worries me."

"Where is this going?" Jinnai frowned.

"I wonder if you remember that box with a picture of a fin whale on it."

"Yeah, I remember it," Jinnai said. He also remembered that Eve had been very attached to it.

"Well, should someone set fire to the house, that box would

burn with it. Before that happens, I wonder if I could impose on you to retrieve it."

"You really are obsessed with that stool, aren't you?"

"It is not a stool!" Eve said with a flash of anger. "And I am not obsessed. I just..."

Now her face was definitely redder. It wasn't just the light, then. And there was something else about the way she was acting today, the things she said—at times he found it hard to grasp their import. The thought processes of an automaton were ultimately opaque in some ways.

"Well..."

There was no getting around it: sneaking into a place known to be dangerous was not a wise practice.

Eve frowned at Jinnai's reluctance. "Very well," she said. "I withdraw my request. I will retrieve the box myself."

She stood up to leave. After a moment's thought, Jinnai said, "Wait. I'll do it."

What was he saying? Did he have a soft spot for her that even he was unaware of?

"But you'll owe me a favor afterward. And I can't guarantee it'll go as planned."

Eve nodded eagerly.

Jinnai had half expected that the Kugimiya residence would be full of hazardous karakuri and booby traps, but Eve insisted that it held nothing of the sort.

Fortunately, it was a new moon. The silent streets around the Kugimiya residence were shrouded in darkness.

Back in his shinobi garb, Jinnai kept a wary eye out for any sign of company as he approached the property.

Since meeting Kyuzo and Eve, his luck had gone from bad to worse. He had never imagined that he would spend so much of his time breaking into buildings dressed as a shinobi.

Keeping his breath shallow, Jinnai entered the main residence.

The box should still be where he had seen it last, in the inner room where Kyuzo spoke to his guests. Jinnai just had to find it, carry it out of the house, and lug it safely back to the bathhouse.

Eve had made a burglar of him. He chuckled at the thought of how far he had fallen.

But when he pushed the sliding door aside and slipped stealthily into the inner room, the smile on his face froze.

"Jinnai. Where have you been hiding?"

The voice was Kihachi's.

Jinnai was astonished. From outside the door, just a yard or two away, he had sensed nothing at all. Now the room was overflowing with murderous intent.

Kihachi was sitting cross-legged on the very box Jinnai had come to steal. It really was just the right height.

"You seem to be laboring under a few misunderstandings," Kihachi said. "Let me set you straight. The shogun's spies work for the shogun. We might find other means of support, but everything we do has to be for the shogun's benefit."

Jinnai sensed several other men appearing outside the room like ghosts. Kihachi's most trusted henchmen, no doubt.

"Let's get back on the right foot. Tell me about the master

of the Conch and Taiko. What does he know, and what is he planning?"

Jinnai hesitated. Kihachi was telling the truth. Those within the shogun's intelligence service tended to wag their tails for whoever paid their bills, but ultimately they were spies for the shogun.

Kihachi was trying to make Jinnai into a mole, just like the Conch and Taiko had done to Kyuzo. Jinnai would continue to feign loyalty to Lord Haga while conveying all his secrets to Kihachi. And if the time came to finish them, Jinnai would ensure that Kihachi had the evidence he needed.

If he accepted Kihachi's proposal, things probably wouldn't go badly for him. He might even end up one of Kihachi's most prized assets.

But Jinnai shook his head.

Even he did not understand why. The old Jinnai would have obeyed without question.

Kihachi sighed. "Have it your way. I saw real potential in you, Jinnai. But this is where your story ends."

The men closing in on Jinnai from behind made it clear that Kihachi was speaking of more than his career in the service.

VI

A few days after Jinnai's disappearance during his visit to the Kugimiya residence, word of the empress's death began going around Tempu.

Kasuga scanned a broadside from a street corner vendor for details. Maintaining the deception must have finally become too difficult even for the imperial household.

Things would finally cool down now. She could start working toward her original goals again.

They say that art can save your life, and it had certainly saved Kasuga and her companion. With Kyuzo Kugimiya vouching for them, they had secured positions in the acrobat troupe currently performing at Nakasu Kannon, alongside the karakuri floats that Kyuzo had built long ago—although Kasuga's unexpected popularity as a performer had brought some problems of its own.

Today's show had been canceled out of respect for the deceased empress. Leaving Nakasu Kannon, Kasuga had just set foot on Ten-Span Bridge when she saw a woman in a red kosode coming toward her.

She had never seen the woman before, but she felt as if lightning had run down her spine.

She's another one. Just like the empress.

Kyuzo Kugimiya was the real thing.

Which meant the empress could be saved...

Kasuga's breast burned with excitement. She felt tears well in her eyes, but the other woman had the coldest look she had ever seen.

The woman stopped a few steps before her. "You must be Kasuga, former lady of the innermost sanctum," she said.

People streamed around them in both directions.

"Kugimiya sent me here to meet you. You and—" the woman paused, then shook her head slowly. "The imperial automaton."

"Jinnai. Out."

Jinnai had been bound in a leaning-forward lotus position and left lying on the floor. With a grunt, he wriggled around so that he could look up.

One of Kihachi's henchmen was grinning down at him through a hatch in the ceiling.

"How do you expect me to get out like this?" Jinnai demanded.

"Still healthy enough to complain, I see. Here." A knife sailed down from the ceiling to land with a splash in the pool of feces and urine that covered the floor. "You do the rest. I'll be back once you're ready."

Jinnai was at Tempu Castle, a guest of the head gardener.

To be specific, he was in the tank under Kihachi's toilet seat.

It was spacious as these things went—perhaps six feet on every side, the size of a small room. The bones on the floor suggested that he was not the first to be imprisoned there.

Jinnai squirmed across the slick floor and managed to catch the dagger between his teeth and use it to cut his bonds.

"Looks like I'll be spared your fate," he said to a maggoty skull nearby.

But *why* was he getting out?

"Lord Haga, master of the Conch and Taiko, has been ordered to commit seppuku," said Kihachi.

Jinnai listened cautiously, the worst of the effluent scrubbed off him.

"I understand he was meeting with a senior palace attendant *without* the shogun's knowledge," Kihachi continued.

Just as Jinnai had feared, their man on the inside had told all. He should have killed him when he had the chance.

Kihachi was carefully pruning the potted plants in his own private yard with a pair of shears.

Jinnai looked down at his own hands. Both little fingers and his left ring finger had been severed at the root. His left hamstring and several toes on his left foot were also gone, as was his left ear.

All had been removed by the very shears Kihachi was using now. He kept them very sharp.

"There's more," Kihachi said. "The Haga household has been dissolved, and the bureau of the Conch and Taiko itself is to be abolished."

Secret meetings with a palace official were bad enough. To attack imperial guards and carriage bearers and kidnap a female official was an outrage.

Placing the shears on a table with a clink, Kihachi accepted a bucket of water from a nearby henchman and dipped a ladle into it to water his plants. Each of them had been tended with loving care for years, and he put them on display around the castle when the season was right.

"You said the empress died too," Jinnai said.

"Yes, and our stubborn prince Hiruhiko has finally agreed to the shogun's demands. It won't be long before a new empress takes the throne."

When she did, the imperial household would be fully absorbed by the shogunate.

Jinnai had his doubts.

The imperial family had kept its secret for three long decades since the empress's birth. Why abandon it so easily now? Hadn't the whole point been to prevent a coup from without like the one that was about to take place?

And then something occurred to him.

What exactly was the "carelessness" Kasuga had committed? More to the point—

Jinnai pushed the thought away. Had he been misunderstanding the whole affair, right from the start?

"You won't be doing much shinobi work in your state," Kihachi told him. "Your master in the Conch and Taiko is dead. You're out of the intelligence service, of course. And your name's been struck off the census lists, too."

In other words, the moment Jinnai set foot outside Tempu Castle, he would be homeless and destitute. A nonperson.

"We're letting you go without killing you in honor of the new empress," said Kihachi with his usual beatific smile. "That's the story, anyway. I'll level with you: I just didn't want to let you rot down there. You think a toilet smells bad without a cadaver in it..."

Kihachi made a show of grimacing, then turned back to his plants and tossed another ladle of water over them.

Kicked out of Tempu Castle in grimy clothes with a rope for an obi, Jinnai made straight for the Kugimiya residence.

He had no shoes or undergarments, and his unusual appearance was enough to keep the other people on the street away.

As he walked, Jinnai's mind raced.

If he was right about his new realization, he had been misreading the situation from the moment he attacked the palanquin at the crossroads.

An icy, silent rain began to fall. Just the thing for his current mood. Tramping down the increasingly muddy road barefoot, Jinnai finally arrived at Kyuzo's compound.

He ducked through the little gate in the walls of raised earth and knocked on the front door.

"Jin?"

Eve appeared from within and hurried to support him when she saw he was on the verge of collapse.

"You were alive, then," she said.

"Turns out you don't owe me one after all," Jinnai said. "Was the stool okay?"

"The what? Oh... Yes. Perfectly safe."

She seemed to want to say more, but didn't.

"Let me tend your wounds inside," she said instead.

"No, they aren't that serious," Jinnai said, stepping into the entryway and sitting down on the step. "I'd like some water, though. And there's someone I want to see."

Eve brought him a cup of water, and he drained it in one gulp.

"She is here, isn't she?" he said. "The imperial automaton."

Eve's expression changed noticeably.

Jinnai added, "The one I thought was Kasuga."

VII

"Astonishing. Master Keian made this himself?"

Kyuzo reached up to rotate a segment of the scope over his eye, adjusting the focus of the thick lenses.

He stood over a slim torso that rested on a workbench at the center of the room. The torso's limbs had been removed and now rested on four smaller, narrower benches arranged around it. Each remained connected to the torso by hundreds of individual strands running to each limb, from hairlike filaments to conduits as thick as a thumb, gathered into bundles that drooped between the benches.

More startling was the head, which sat on a slightly raised platform of its own, connected by another mass of tubes and wires.

The chestnut-colored, slightly wavy hair that Kasuga loved

had been cropped short, as befit a kamuro. Given the empress's childlike features, the effect was not without its charm.

The empress's eyes were closed. Apart from the occasional twitch of her eyelids, she looked fast asleep.

We know what you are, Kasuga. You are an ukami.

That night in the innermost sanctum, the empress had seen through her facade. And in that moment, Kasuga had made her decision.

She would not, could not, ever lie to the empress again. Automaton or not, this was the woman to whom she had sworn her life in service.

Kasuga was the daughter of the master of ukami. On her twelfth birthday, Prince Hiruhiko himself had informed her of the empress's secret and assigned her to the innermost sanctum to determine if any of the other girls had discovered the truth.

She listened closely to their conversations both on and off duty. Sometimes, in the attendants' quarters, she joined their discussions to ask a probing question. Whenever any of the others hinted at knowing more than they should, she told the prince and they were killed.

Even for someone who had been training as an ukami since birth, to inform on fellow attendants, on friends, knowing that they would be put to death, was near-unbearable at times. This was when Kasuga poured her heart and soul into her everyday duties for the empress, striving to perform even the tiniest detail with the utmost care. The more deeply she venerated the empress, the more trivial everything else seemed. By treating Her Majesty as more than human despite knowing that she was a machine, Kasuga had sought to protect herself.

You are an ukami.

With these words, the empress had finally freed Kasuga from her double life. Kasuga had wept.

Will you protect us?

The ukami served the empress, and the empress needed her now.

Kasuga's resolve was set. Even if it meant making enemies of the entire imperial household, including the other ukami, she would keep the empress safe.

"Our father was a man named Keian Higa, but he has long since departed this life," the empress said.

As a result, she explained, she had not received repairs or maintenance for some time, and her systems were failing one by one.

"Keian operated a private school called the Institute of Machinery. It was closed when his plot against the shogun was uncovered, but one of his students disappeared just before the magistrates made their arrests."

The two of them were beyond the veil on the imperial bed. The empress whispered as if imparting a great secret.

"That student was a mole. Keian knew but feigned ignorance because the student showed such promise."

"And so..."

Even now, Kasuga felt a nervous thrill at breaking the injunction against speaking to the empress directly.

"We think he escaped beheading, and lives still. He is the only one who can repair our person. His name is Kyuzo Kugimiya."

"Am I to bring him to the palace, then?"

The empress slowly shook her head. "No. We will leave the

palace and go to him."

She spoke simply, but the sheer audacity of what she proposed was stunning.

"Leave the palace? But, Your Majesty..." Kasuga's voice trembled with shock.

"We have a plan. You, Kasuga, are the only one who can help us carry it out."

At these words, Kasuga fairly melted with delight.

"Master Kyuzo."

Kasuga's reverie was interrupted when Eve entered the room. Kyuzo did not even look up, so absorbed was he in the construction of the imperial automaton.

Then Kasuga saw the man Eve had brought with her and leapt to her feet, her color rising.

"Wait," the man said. "I'm not here to start anything. You don't need to either."

He looked very different now, but this was definitely the man who had ambushed the palanquin, left Kasuga for dead, and hidden the empress in the Thirteen Floors.

"I'm with the shogun's intelligence service," he said. "Or was. My name is Jinnai Tasaka."

"No fighting in here, either of you," Kyuzo said without looking up. "These are delicate mechanisms."

Kasuga slipped the weighted length of wire back into the fold of her kimono.

"So you were the real Kasuga," said the man who called

himself Jinnai, as if through gritted teeth.

Kasuga had little sympathy for him. He had knocked their plan off-kilter before it had even begun.

It had begun on a night when Kasuga was assigned to the empress's bedchamber. As agreed, the empress had pretended to shut down. Rather than telling the ladies-in-waiting, Kasuga had slipped into Prince Hiruhiko's quarters to inform him.

The prince was already under pressure from the shogunate on the matter of abdication. This did not help matters. Kasuga proposed that they smuggle the empress out of the palace and find a technician to repair her without revealing her identity. They could hide her in the palanquin they used for attendants who had been "careless," and Kasuga could ride along as well.

Meanwhile, within the palace, the word would be spread that the empress's illness had worsened and that she was to be attended only by Kasuga for the time being. No one would know that she had left, and once her maintenance was complete, they would simply eliminate anyone who had been aware of the true situation.

This was Kasuga's proposal, and Prince Hiruhiko had given his assent.

The second, secret part of the plan was for Kasuga to wait until they were a fair distance from the palace and then burst out of the palanquin, kill the guards and porters, then abscond with the empress to Tempu.

But Jinnai had launched his attack on the procession first, and even Kasuga had barely escaped with her life. Worse, he had abducted the empress, leaving a human corpse Kasuga did not recognize in her place.

Thinking quickly, the empress had claimed to be Kasuga when Jinnai had asked and had let him take her to Tempu.

And now all three had been reunited in Kyuzo's workshop.

Kasuga was still glaring at Jinnai when she realized that the empress's eyelids were slowly rising.

Now hear this: the day is come!

She felt a pang of nostalgia for those languorous palace mornings. They would not come again.

"Jinnai," said Kyuzo. "I understand that the Haga line has been ended and the Conch and Taiko dissolved."

Jinnai nodded.

"My own position as refinery assistant might vanish before long, too." Removing the scope from his eye, Kyuzo rose to his feet. Stiff shouldered, perhaps from his work, he tilted his head left and right to crack his neck and began to massage his own shoulders. "The secret is secret no longer; what cards we had are worthless. The shogun's men will have the imperial tomb open before long, I imagine."

Eve frowned. "But that's where..."

"The Sacred Vessel from the Age of Myth slumbers," said the empress's head.

Was the tremble in her voice different from usual? Some side effect of maintenance, perhaps.

Kasuga had pursued the empress's abductors to Tempu, but the trail had gone cold there. She had begun by locating Kyuzo Kugimiya to request his assistance with the imperial automaton's maintenance. Well, not request so much as demand, given the blade at his throat.

But Kyuzo had not shown a hint of fear. On the contrary, he

seemed genuinely interested in the prospect.

When Kasuga heard that Kyuzo had been summoned by the master of the Conch and Taiko and forced to agree to a meeting at the Thirteen Floors with Jinnai and a former lady of the innermost chamber named Kasuga, she was confused for a moment but then realized what must be happening. The empress was concealing her true identity beneath that of her former servant.

And so Kyuzo had good reason not to appear at the meeting as planned.

If Haga and Jinnai learned that their "Kasuga" was actually the empress herself, who had, furthermore, fled from the palace of her own volition, they might have locked her up in the Haga residence forever.

Kyuzo wanted to inspect the imperial automaton for himself. Kasuga wanted her to get the maintenance she needed. The benefits of working together were obvious.

Kasuga had rescued the empress from the Thirteen Floors, but her methods had created new problems.

Kyuzo had gone into hiding, leaving his residence deserted, and Eve had been left in a friendly bathhouse with instructions to help Jinnai.

But the imperial automaton's maintenance could only be performed in Kyuzo's workshop.

And so Kyuzo had entrusted Kasuga and the empress to an acrobat troupe currently at Nakasu Kannon. He had been making karakuri stalls for the temple for some time and was able to call in favors. Kasuga's ukami training let her pose as a member of the troupe without difficulty.

Eventually, they assumed, the palace would no longer be able to conceal the empress's absence. When that happened, the word would go out that she had died or perhaps just abdicated. The heat would die down, the surveillance would be lifted from Kyuzo's residence, and he would finally be able to inspect and repair the empress at his leisure.

All this meant that Jinnai's struggles with Chokichi Yaguruma and the shogun's spies had been utterly pointless. Haga had been ordered to commit seppuku, his family line had been dissolved, and the Conch and Taiko as an organization had been disbanded, just as the shogun had been planning for some time.

"Developed a limp, I see," Kyuzo said. "And you don't seem to have the standard complement of fingers anymore. Or ears." Jinnai didn't smile. "All Eve's fault, of course. She shouldn't have asked you to get her box in the first place. Let me take a look at you later."

"What good will that do? You aren't a physician," said Jinnai.

The corners of Kyuzo's mouth twitched. It was the closest thing to an expression Jinnai had seen on his face since arriving earlier.

"What a physician cannot heal," said Kyuzo, "I can."

VIII

Some days later, when his wounds were finally patched up, Jinnai accompanied Eve across Ten-Span Bridge to Nakasu Kannon.

They had invited Kyuzo, too, but he had shown no interest in joining them.

Jinnai thought back to his parting from Eve at the top of the bridge before leaving for his assignment in Kamigata. Only a few months had passed, but everything had changed. His station in life, and even his body.

He looked down at his hands as they walked. The fingers that should have been missing were all present, good as new.

Long hours of practice had been required before he could walk properly again, but now he could run and jump like anyone else.

"Maybe with these repairs I'll finally understand you," Jinnai said. "I hope so."

"You will never understand me," Eve said with a smile. "Even among humans, the thoughts of another are never truly knowable, are they?"

He had to admit she was right. Humans and automata had that in common.

They crossed the bridge, walked past the stalls and under Bonten Gate, and arrived at the plaza.

The karakuri floats of last time were nowhere to be seen. Now the space was filled with a single gigantic big top.

Four great round posts served as tent poles, and the heavy canvas was pulled taut by ropes in eight directions and held in place by stakes driven into the ground.

A crowd had gathered around the tent flap, and the food vendors were doing a brisk trade. The signs outside the big top depicted gruesome man-beast hybrids, frolicking contortionists, and—proudly displayed in prime position—a young girl doing midair tricks on a wire.

They entered the crowded tent and found Kasuga in the middle of her performance.

Dressed in something filmy that glittered like a celestial maiden's cloak of feathers, she bounded adroitly above a net stretched between the tentpoles. Her weighted wire shot out and sent the flames shooting forth from a row of ten candles to deafening applause. Certainly a better use of her talents than killing.

What caught Jinnai's attention was Kasuga's partner, who was beating a drum in time with the aerial display. Or trying to. Her rhythm was erratic, and he doubted it had any effect other than to distract Kasuga and irritate the crowds. In fact, looking closely Jinnai thought he saw Kasuga trying to adjust her own movements to match the irregular drumbeat.

"Should we stay and speak to them after the show?" asked Eve.

Jinnai thought for a moment. "Let's not," he said.

They exited the tent again, leaving Kasuga in midair and the empress drumming.

On the evening of the following day, when Jinnai accompanied Eve to the temple again for her daily prayers, the troupe had already moved on, leaving nothing in the plaza but an icy winter wind.

PSYCHE ETERNAL

I

"Interesting."

Kihachi Umekawa, master of the Garden of August Repose, was face-to-face with the iron cabinet hidden in the depths of the imperial tomb.

The tomb was a burial mound in the ancient style, located at the center of the pentagonal courtyard that was the heart of the imperial palace. It was topped with a cover of gleaming black iron like an enormous turtle, and the cover was crisscrossed with more recently installed iron scaffolding.

Kihachi gathered that the tomb had been strictly off-limits long before the palace had been rebuilt over it, but the precautions that had been taken to secure it were unusually extreme.

How the cover had been installed, nobody knew. Kihachi's men had needed over a hundred days to pierce it. It concealed a large stone cavern that smelled of mold, and in the cavern was the iron cabinet.

Ten workmen were in the cavern with him, and preparations to extract the cabinet were underway.

Kihachi held his gando lantern high, illuminating the cabinet. It was perhaps six feet square at the base and at least nine feet high. The lower part was carved with some kind of diagram that covered every square inch of the surface.

According to Lord Fujibayashi, governor of Saumi, who headed the refinery and had inspected the cabinet first, it was unclear how these designs had been executed or how the cabinet itself had been sealed.

Kihachi looked up. Above him he saw the hole punched in the tomb's cover. Through the hole the scaffolding was visible, and beyond that a cloudless blue sky.

Satisfied that the preparations had been made as planned, Kihachi climbed a ladder out of the tomb.

In the courtyard, Kihachi's gardeners—in other words, the shogun's spies—mingled with laborers from the refinery as they bustled around various workstations. The project was top secret, and most of the necessary muscle had been brought in from Tempu.

Mounts of leftover soil and work tools lay scattered around, and several lean-tos had been thrown together to provide shade. The elegance and languor one might expect at the imperial palace was entirely absent. It looked like a construction site.

The shogun's men had been solicitous of the palace's inhabitants at first, but now they tramped through the place like they owned it. Kihachi gathered that there had been irritating conventions to observe in the past, but the stricter the rule, the faster it crumbled once broken. It was only a matter of time before they had free rein even of the inner rooms, theoretically restricted to those of noble birth, and even the inner sanctum where the empress dwelled.

At Kihachi's signal, his gardeners scrambled up the scaffolding and attached a dozen hefty pulleys to the scaffolding around the opening. The pulleys, so enormous that each man could only carry one, were wound with the special kind of rope made of human hair that temples used to hang their bells. When each rope was securely wrapped around its pulley, its free end was tossed down through the hole in the imperial tomb's ceiling to be tied around the cabinet.

Kihachi watched the network of ropes take form, like an enormous spiderweb spun over the tomb. Finally, a man approached to tell him that everything was in place.

"Begin," Kihachi told him.

"Third time's the charm, eh, Kihachi?" said Fujibayashi, sitting on a portable bench in the shade of a large parasol.

"I hope so, milord."

This would be their third attempt to hoist the cabinet from its chamber of stone. The first had failed when the cabinet proved too heavy to lift. The second time around, they had raised it six or seven feet off the ground before the rope snapped and the men underneath were crushed. If the web of ropes and pulleys failed, they would have to take a different approach altogether. As the man charged with getting the cabinet out, Kihachi's professional reputation was at stake.

The ends of the ropes that came down the sides of the tomb

had been gathered into four bundles. At Kihachi's signal, the men in the courtyard divided into four groups. Each took up one of the bundles and began to pull, slowly backing away from the imperial tomb.

At first the glossy black rope only stretched, with the cabinet obstinately immobile.

Kihachi made a noise of disgust. *Another failure.*

But then, slowly, the cabinet began to rise.

By now the ropes were stretched to half their original thickness. Their elasticity made them stronger.

The tip of the cabinet's hip-and-gable roof showed through the hole in the iron dome. Men up on the scaffolding stopped the cabinet from swaying and guided it up through the hole, which was just barely large enough for it.

Kihachi swallowed. This was where the rope had snapped last time.

But this time they had more pulleys and better rope, and soon the entire cabinet was clear. They waited for the men still in the tomb to emerge, then laid thick square logs across the hole in the dome, covering it completely.

The plan was to lower the cabinet onto the logs, untie the ropes, and then build a ramp of rock and earth to carefully slide the cabinet down to ground level. The work of opening it would begin after that.

But.

Even though they had chosen oak and cherry and other hard timbers, as soon as the cabinet came to rest on the logs, they started to creak and break.

"Hold firm!" Kihachi yelled at the men still holding the ropes.

But when they hurriedly pulled the ropes taut again, the cabinet was yanked off-balance.

Before Kihachi could react, it had toppled onto its side and begun sliding down the black dome with increasing speed.

The pulleys were torn free of their moorings and flew into the air. Some of the men holding the ropes went with them.

Kihachi grabbed Fujibayashi by the collar and dragged him back, away from the tomb.

An instant later, the tumbling iron cabinet slammed into the ground right where they had just been, skidding to a stop in a spray of earth and dust.

Kihachi glanced over at Fujibayashi. He was white as a sheet but unharmed.

The courtyard was in an uproar. The men yanked into the air by the ropes they'd been holding had landed on their heads and now twitched horribly on the ground. Others groaned and bled where they lay, having failed to get out of the cabinet's path in time.

Ignoring them all, Kihachi hurried to the cabinet.

Part of its roof was cracked.

Kihachi smiled internally.

If all had gone as planned today, building the ramp to get the cabinet down would have taken weeks, and who knew how much longer would have been needed to get the thing open. This accident had accomplished both tasks in seconds. If the price for that was a few gardeners and refinery laborers, so be it.

Suddenly, a small moving object sprang out of the crack in the roof. Without thinking, Kihachi caught it in his hands.

He felt something jumping between his cupped palms.

Waiting until it calmed down somewhat, he opened his hands a crack to peer inside.

He was holding a single cricket, its antennae trembling.

A good omen. He transferred the insect to a bamboo tube he produced from the front fold of his work clothes. He carried the tubes with him everywhere at this time of year, along with insect cages, in case he spotted a cricket while working in the castle gardens. With the excavations at the palace, he had resigned himself to not finding an entrant for the tournament this year.

The palace grounds were the original home of cricket fighting, before it had spread to the common folk. A cricket caught here would have to be a good one.

The question of how an insect could emerge alive from a sealed cabinet in a tomb left undisturbed for decades did nag at him, but he supposed the creature must have found its way into the cavern and hidden in the carvings on the cabinet's panels.

Tucking the bamboo tube back into his work clothes, Kihachi began barking orders across the still-chaotic courtyard.

II

"I wonder if Kyuzo will ever build Tentoku a new body."

Jinnai turned to look at Eve, sitting beside him on the rear veranda of the Kugimiya residence. He saw the gleam of tears beneath her long lashes.

It had been more than ten years since he had first spoken to her at Nakasu Kannon, but she was as young and beautiful as ever.

"One thing I've learned from my time here is how deep the art of automata is," he said. "A wrestler's body can't be an easy thing to make, although admittedly I didn't know the man in life."

"In life!" Eve looked at him sharply. "You speak as though he were dead."

Jinnai shook his head hurriedly. "A slip of the tongue," he said. "Forgive me."

"Will you ask Kyuzo about Tentoku for me, when he returns?"

"All right, all right."

With a sigh, Eve got to her feet and withdrew into the house. He must have upset her.

Thinking of Tentoku's life captured and preserved inside a wooden box, Jinnai surveyed the yard. It was as unbeautiful as ever: an expanse of hardened earth without a single tree or even a decorative rock.

Ten years. It felt like a single moment.

On the surface, the world appeared more peaceful now. Not long after the dissolution of the Conch and Taiko, Kyuzo had been relieved of his post at the refinery. Nevertheless, he had retained his residence on the outskirts of Tempu, and Jinnai, with nowhere else to go after losing his own job with the shogun's intelligence service, had moved in as a live-in apprentice, learning the art of automata. Before long Kyuzo was running something of a private school.

He did not have many students, but he admitted not only those with some experience in mechanics but also the children of daimyo and *hatamoto* from distant domains (if they showed potential), samurai stationed in Tempu, and even ronin.

The Kugimiya residence was much busier these days as a result, but as far as Jinnai knew, none of the students had even guessed that the diligent Eve was in fact the pinnacle of the art they studied.

Jinnai rose to his feet and followed the stepping-stones across the yard to the workshop. He was the only student permitted inside, but this was simply because he already knew so much that there was no reason to hide anything from him.

Jinnai passed through the workshop's two doors, removed his sandals, and stepped up onto the wooden floor. The basement of the storehouse room was where Kyuzo performed maintenance on Eve's person and other tasks he did not wish anyone to see, but this was not Jinnai's destination today. He walked past the eternal clock in the middle of the main room and entered a smaller room at the back of the building.

The rear room contained a workbench, much smaller than Kyuzo's, on which lay the golden macaw, opened to the throat.

Jinnai sat down beside it, fixed the scope to one eye, and got to work.

The bird was an automaton that Kyuzo had made as an experiment when he had been a student at Keian Higa's Institute of Machinery. Its skin was adorned with real, colorful feathers, but its innards were not flesh and bone but springs, clockwork, and gears arranged within a dully gleaming skeleton carved of metal.

The balance wheel where its heart should be was currently still.

When Jinnai learned that Kyuzo had made the macaw simply by copying existing designs, Jinnai had been too stunned to speak.

Beside the workbench stood a lacquered box with mother-of-pearl inlay and a tree branch sticking out of it. This was the true "body" of the automaton; it contained the workings that set the bird in motion and gave it the appearance of life.

Kyuzo had not been skillful enough at the time to fit everything inside the macaw itself. He had begun as a craftsman for the karakuri floats at Nakasu Kannon, and the macaw represented the last remnants of those techniques.

Today, Kyuzo dismissed the bird as a toy, but the more Jinnai examined it, the greater the gulf between the two of them felt. Certainly he doubted whether he could re-create the bird himself.

But this was all part of his training. Kyuzo had ordered him to determine what was wrong with the macaw and fix it by himself. He would not even tell Jinnai what had caused the bird to begin malfunctioning several days before. He had never been a very hands-on teacher.

Jinnai was not quite ready to begin disassembling the bird, fearing that if he took it apart at his current level, he would never get it back together again. He continued his inspection, rotating the dial on his monocular scope to bring the lens into focus on each new component.

Soon he felt himself beginning to perspire. The work took staggering amounts of concentration, and if he failed to take plenty of breaks, it soon gave him a headache severe enough to take him out of commission for an hour. Ten years into his studies, he had yet to get used to this.

If Kyuzo was left to his own devices, he could work for two days, even three, without sleeping, eating, or even drinking.

Jinnai gave up and rose to his feet.

Shinobi training with the intelligence service had been easy compared to this.

"What I hear is, since the death of Gobo-in, the palace has been full of men from the refinery."

Sashichi peered down at the washing area of the bathhouse as he spoke, a serious expression on his face.

"Is that so?" Jinnai said. He poured himself another cup of sake and took a thoughtful sip.

Perhaps because today was both the Ebisu-ko Festival and a gift day, the mezzanine above the changing area was even livelier than usual. Games of go and shogi were in progress. Some customers were gambling, while others, like Jinnai, were simply enjoying a drink after their bath.

Sashichi was the second son of the Arita family, designated emissaries to Tempu from the Utsuki domain. Sashichi was a samurai by rank, but his older brother had already inherited the main family line, leaving Sashichi to a life of leisurely dissipation. The family had bundled him off to Kyuzo's school at the age of thirty to get him out of their hair.

He could be impulsive, and it showed, but he wasn't malicious. He had a way with people and a knack for automata, which seemed to suit his nature.

"I also hear there's been no smoke from the refinery chimneys in quite some time."

"Oh? Why's that?"

"Just between you and me, the word is that the Sacred Vessel from the Age of Myth has been dug up." To judge from his tone, all of Kyuzo's other students had heard the rumor already.

If enough people were on a project together, word was bound to get out.

"Kyuzo must have been summoned to the castle to inspect their find," Jinnai muttered, as if to himself.

Several days ago, Lord Fujibayashi, governor of Saumi and head of the refinery, had come to see Kyuzo for the first time since dismissing him from his position as assistant.

Jinnai doubted the shogunate had decided that Kyuzo was trustworthy after all. If they were drafting him into their project anyway, something remarkable must be afoot.

Kyuzo had left Jinnai with instructions to watch over his household but had given him no information about why he was going to the castle or when he would be back.

In fact, Kyuzo had ordered Jinnai not to investigate any further, but this sat poorly with Jinnai's nature, and Eve seemed worried too. So Jinnai had been casually questioning all of the other students with some connection to the shogunate, however slight. Today it was Sashichi's turn.

"Hey, there's Eve," said Sashichi, still watching the washing area.

Eve always visited the bathhouse on gift days bearing a generous twist of cash. This had not changed in all the years Jinnai had known her.

"Beautiful as ever," Sashichi sighed.

Jinnai craned his neck and saw Eve's pale form through the steam below. The men in the washing room noticed her too, and their eyes followed her restlessly as she passed. Some forgot themselves and watched so intently that they earned themselves a swift thwack on the head with a wooden bucket from their wives.

"There's something about that woman," Sashichi said. "The contrast between those cool looks and the strange way she acts sometimes—the odd things she says and does. Makes her even more appealing."

"I'd put her out of your mind if I were you," said Jinnai wryly, pulling the panel over the peephole closed.

"Of course, I'd never lay a hand on Master Kyuzo's only daughter," said Sashichi. "But she makes my lover's blood sing. A woman like that you can't ignore." He shrugged.

That wasn't quite what Jinnai had been getting at, but like the rest of Kyuzo's students, Sashichi had no idea what Eve truly was. The truth would probably knock him off his feet.

"Getting back to our earlier conversation," Jinnai said, pouring Sashichi another drink.

"The Sacred Vessel? It'd be intriguing if they really had found it. It's supposed to have been kept in the innermost sanctum of the palace for years, but rumor has it that the Vessel incorporates the finest technology there is. Mechanics, chemistry, electricity—you name it."

This appeared to be the limits of Sashichi's knowledge. Jinnai pondered the situation.

It had been ten years since the death of the previous empress had been announced not long after she'd gone missing.

The current empress had ascended to the throne as an infant, so her father, Prince Hiruhiko, had renamed himself "Gobo-in," assumed the privileges of a retired empress for himself, and continued his regency without interruption.

But then, six months earlier, Gobo-in had succumbed to the palsy and died.

What is Eve doing here?

That was Kyuzo's first thought when he saw the sleeping form. He even wondered if this was some kind of joke, but Fujibayashi and the unpleasant-looking men behind him who were there to keep an eye on Kyuzo were unsmiling.

"This is the Sacred Vessel from the Age of Myth," said Fujibayashi. "Newly extracted from the imperial tomb."

Kyuzo put his hand to his chin and surveyed their find, which lay naked on the workbench.

Closed, long-lashed eyes. Lips like a flower about to bloom. Eve's twin in every particular.

"You may find this hard to believe," Fujibayashi added, lowering his voice, "but it is actually a karakuri doll."

Very few people knew how advanced Keian Higa's work had been or what Kyuzo was doing to continue it. Fujibayashi was clearly among the vast majority who had no idea that an automaton could talk and move like a person.

"Does it work?" Kyuzo asked.

Fujibayashi shook his head. "At first we thought it was the remains of some ancient noble who had somehow escaped putrefaction, but—"

"Those details are irrelevant. I asked you if it works."

"It does not," Fujibayashi said icily. "That is why you are here."

Kyuzo nodded, shrugging off his silk crepe jacket and pushing it into the hands of one of the men behind Fujibayashi.

"Is there a magnifying scope?" he asked.

"There should be all the tools and materials you need. If anything is lacking, let us know," said Fujibayashi. He had one of his men bring Kyuzo a scope from a corner shelf.

Fitting the scope to his eye like a monocle, Kyuzo leaned over the Vessel's face. He pushed its right eyelid open with his finger to reveal eyes of dark green. Agate green.

Kyuzo gestured for someone to hand him a candle, then experimentally moved it back and forth before the eye. No change.

A mechanism in Eve's eyes used wafers of a certain precious stone to open and close radially arranged metal wings behind the pupil depending on light conditions. He saw what appeared to be a similar mechanism in the Vessel's eyes, but it remained inert.

He pulled up the Vessel's top lip. Its teeth were smooth and gleaming and beautifully even. They were made using pearl oyster shells, just like Eve's.

After a moment's thought, Kyuzo set about detaching the Vessel's limbs.

Gripping an elbow, he brought the hand of that arm around to the armpit, then twisted the joint in the opposite direction to dislocate it. Here, too, the mechanism and even the angles were the same as Eve's. After removing the other arm in the same way, he twisted the legs outward to dislocate them too, so that all four of the Vessel's limbs were dangling at disturbing angles from the workbench.

He heard Fujibayashi swallow behind him.

"Are there no other benches?" demanded Kyuzo. Several more were hurriedly brought in, and he arranged the limbs on them so that the automaton appeared to be spreading her arms and legs wide.

Then he took a pair of shears from the tool shelf and began cutting into the Vessel's skin.

The other men in the room averted their eyes. The cruelty of the sight must have been too much for them. But no blood welled from the incisions, and no meat or sinew was revealed. Only bundle after bundle of dully gleaming wires and tubes numbering in the thousands.

Once the four limbs were completely separated from the torso, Kyuzo returned to the Vessel's head. He seized it by the hair and shook it briskly as his other hand disengaged the connection with a practiced motion under the jaw.

The assembled watchers exhaled a collective sigh at the deftness of his work.

Detailed inspection of the Vessel's internal structure would be needed, but at this point Kyuzo had encountered nothing that differed from Eve in any way. Although his face remained impassive, he found it difficult to understand.

Kyuzo placed the head on the bench that had been prepared for it and turned to Fujibayashi.

"My task is to make it work?"

"If you can."

"My inspection may uncover components requiring maintenance. The materials needed may be rare or expensive. I assume you have no objection?"

But this project was being funded by the shogunate. Presumably money was no object.

So thinking, Kyuzo turned back to the disassembled Vessel.

III

"Agitate the competitors," the referee said.

The two crickets were in a fighting basin of unglazed pottery. It was oval in shape, five inches long and seven across, and partitioned by a sheet of paper across the middle that kept the two crickets from making contact too early.

At the referee's signal, the cricket trainers in both corners began stroking their own insect's antennae with a *senso*—a narrow brush made of mouse whiskers and rice stem fibers. The crickets, which had been sitting calmly in their corners, became increasingly irritated. Skillful use of the senso was interpreted by the strongly territorial male crickets as a challenge, firing up their fighting spirit.

By now both crickets were roaming their half of the basin, searching for the intruder that had touched their antennae.

Jinnai watched from the sidelines thoughtfully. People said that senso technique decided one-tenth of the outcome. And it was harder than it looked to enrage an insect and get it into the mood to fight instead of just scaring it. Even the best cricket could lose to an inferior-ranked opponent if its prefight senso didn't do the job.

"Begin!" said the referee.

An official in formal kimono and hakama removed the paper partition.

The cricket in the east corner, slightly blue in color, immediately sprang onto the pale cricket in the west corner. A roar went up from the spectators crowded around the table to watch.

It was rare for a cricket to close in so quickly. Normally the two insects would size each other up for a short period before the fight began in earnest.

But this was the grand tournament held by the shogun himself. Only the strongest fighters from each domain were entered. They really were of a different breed entirely than the crickets used by the townspeople, Jinnai mused.

The blue cricket was like a mad dog. The white cricket retained its composure, feinting once before biting into the other's abdomen.

This was not normal cricket behavior either. Most of them aimed for their opponents' mandibles or the weak spot at their neck. Jinnai had never seen one go for the abdomen before.

It must have realized that letting the blue cricket come straight for it would put it at a disadvantage and had gone on the offensive instead to knock its opponent off guard. If so, it had worked: the blue cricket backed off and watched to see what the white cricket would do next. This might be the first time it had been bitten on the abdomen.

Jinnai did not really believe that the insects themselves thought in these terms, but watching from the sidelines, it was the natural interpretation of their actions.

Now that both crickets had shown that they were ready to fight, they stared each other down, neither showing the other its rear in retreat.

"Agitate the competitors."

The senso came out again as the crickets slowly circled each other inside the basin. The referee could call for the senso to be used again after the bout had begun, but it was not permitted otherwise.

As soon as the blue cricket's trainer touched its antennae, the cricket kicked off with its rear legs and leapt toward the white cricket again.

The white cricket reacted swiftly, jumping back an inch. The blue cricket landed off-balance, and the white cricket saw its opportunity and sank its mandibles into its opponent's neck.

The crowd around the fighting basin roared again.

Keeping its jaws firmly in the blue cricket's neck, the white cricket twisted its entire body to the side. The two insects tumbled together into the middle of the basin.

The blue cricket opened its wings in a desperate attempt to regain its feet, but its opponent tossed it from side to side with unbelievable strength given its size. Before long, the blue cricket slowly drew in its wings in apparent submission.

"Enough!"

The referee raised his baton toward the west corner, and the two insects were separated. The blue cricket fled to the edge of the basin, keeping its back to its opponent. The white cricket stayed where it was, scraping its wings together in triumphant stridulation.

The gathered spectators began to talk animatedly among themselves. The referee wrote something on a strip of paper and handed it to the trainer in the west corner. The one in the east corner used a small net to capture the blue cricket and return it to its habitat, then trudged out of the room.

The last bout of the morning was over.

The room had four other tables, each with its own official. Jinnai stepped out into the corridor and the constant stream of people coming and going. He passed another room so full that people were spilling out into the hallway. Realizing that Sashichi was among them, he clapped the younger man on the shoulder.

Sashichi's eyes widened. "Jinnai! Where have you been?" He was carrying several cricket habitats in a box.

"Thought I'd take in a bout while I was here. Very different from the cricket fights I've seen in gambling houses."

"I should hope so!" Sashichi said with a frown. "That's just bug sumo. This is the real thing."

Utsuki domain had sent many crickets to the shogunal tournament over the years, and Sashichi had been called on to serve his domain as a senso technician. In his younger days, his interest in crickets had exceeded even his interest in women, and he had sunk a fortune into the pastime. He considered himself a more serious person today but still admitted to a twinge of excitement when autumn was in the air.

"Did you finish your weigh-in?" asked Jinnai.

"Bit of a delay," Sashichi said, pointing into the room to the head of the line.

There were four tables with balance scales for weighing competitors, but only one was currently manned. Not enough staff on hand, perhaps.

"The shogun's cricket jumped out of the weighing basket and escaped."

"It did, did it? Hawk and Plum, right?"

"Yes. No one dared move in case they stepped on it."

The shogun himself entered a competitor in the grand tournament. The entire shogunate began its cricket-hunting operation in spring and carried on through summer. They also bought the best insects from private dealers and received many as donations as well, since the donor of a cricket that made it into the tournament received a significant cash reward. These were cared for by the officials who ran the whole tournament, so the quality of their upbringing was unimpeachable.

The sheer amount of time, money, and effort invested by the shogunate meant that its crickets were always strong competitors, but Hawk and Plum was said to be on an entirely different level.

"They did catch it, though?"

"That's what they're weighing right now," Sashichi said, pointing at the official adjusting the weights on his balance scale.

"At this rate they won't get everyone weighed and start the bouts until evening."

Sashichi nodded. "I'd say so."

For Jinnai, the longer all this was drawn out, the better.

The grand cricket-fighting tournament was the one chance a year the domains had to pit their finest crickets against each other in the presence of the shogun himself.

The shogun, naturally, was granted prime position before the fighting basin. This meant that the trainers whose crickets were competing stood at the same table as the shogun himself—a great honor for a warrior.

But only ten trainers each year enjoyed this honor, because only the final five bouts were viewed by the shogun. Those bouts would be held a few days from now. Sashichi was there for the preliminary rounds that whittled the many hopefuls down to that final ten. And Jinnai was there as his assistant.

His true interest, of course, had nothing to do with crickets.

Infiltrating Tempu Castle by stealth was no easy task, and not even official domain emissaries could come and go as they pleased. The tournament was just the excuse Jinnai needed, and Sashichi's connection to Utsuki and his complete trust of Jinnai were also helpful.

Jinnai left Sashichi waiting in line and headed outside.

The castle was filled with unfamiliar visitors in the days before the tournament, which allowed Jinnai to roam the grounds with relative freedom. Certain key areas were off-limits, of course, like the central courtyard where the castle keep stood, but when he emerged into the yard, he found it full of rural samurai strolling around taking in the scenery, just as he was.

Jinnai had not been back to the castle since Kihachi had cast him out onto the streets a decade ago, but he remembered it well. Feigning the same idleness as the other sightseers, he walked through the grounds trying to get a sense of where Kyuzo might be—just in case. He had already checked the refinery but had found no sign of anything unusual afoot there.

Soon Jinnai's attention was caught by a small grove of pine trees in the lower western courtyard. Beyond them stood a small cluster of storehouses—the armory, the arsenal, and so on. But the path that way was blocked by a bamboo barrier.

Jinnai did not imagine that anyone would show much interest in the plum trees since it was not the season for them to blossom, but there was the barrier, more than thirty yards wide. Not unclimbable, but certainly intended to keep people away. And so recently made that the bamboo was still green.

Feigning indifference, Jinnai turned and walked in another direction. He soon found that all the other paths leading to the lower western courtyard were blocked in the same way.

It was the only area blocked off like that, at least in the parts of the castle grounds accessible to visitors. If Kyuzo was here, he had to be in one of those storehouses.

"Jinnai! Is that you? What are you doing here?"

Jinnai had completed his circuit and was just making his way back to the building when the voice came from overhead. Looking up, he saw Kihachi Umekawa on a ladder leaning against a black pine.

"Nothing," Jinnai replied with the hint of a smile.

Kihachi was acting as if he had happened to catch sight of Jinnai while pruning some old leaves, but Jinnai knew there was no way that was true.

Knowing that he could not square off against Kihachi directly, Jinnai had intentionally visited during the tournament season to at least make it difficult for Kihachi to move against him.

"Hold the ladder, would you?" said Kihachi. "It wobbles."

Jinnai hesitated but then did as he was asked. He doubted that Kihachi would try anything right there.

Kihachi descended the ladder, looking at Jinnai's hands curiously.

"You have an octopus in your family tree? Or a lizard, maybe?"

"What does that mean?"

"Your fingers have grown back. And your legs are..."

He seemed to be genuinely curious, not laying a trap. It was a rare expression to see on his face.

Jinnai smiled wryly. "No octopus blood, but my great-grand-father was a crab."

Kihachi frowned. "Not funny," he said. "Well, you look like you're in good health, anyway. What are you doing these days?"

Jinnai chose his answer with care. "As you know, I'm just a simple karakuri maker's apprentice now."

"And what business does a trainee puppeteer have in Tempu Castle?"

"I came to look for my master, who seems to have disappeared," Jinnai said innocently. "I hope nothing terrible has happened to him."

Kihachi made a small noise of irritation. Jinnai decided to change the subject.

"I hear the shogun's put forth a remarkable contender at this year's cricket-fighting tournament," he said. "Hawk and Plum, was it? They say it eats its opponents alive. Everyone else is in a cold sweat, hoping they won't have to meet it in the brackets."

"What's your point, Jinnai?" Kihachi asked darkly.

"Well, there's a rumor that Hawk and Plum was discovered

inside the imperial palace."

And that wasn't all. By tradition, each cricket's fighting name included part of the name of its discoverer.

And Umekawa meant "Plum River."

"Some people even say it crawled out of the imperial tomb."

"You'll take years off your life talking like this, Jinnai."

That, it seemed, was Kihachi's reply.

If the cricket had been found in the imperial tomb and presented to the shogun by Kihachi, that was proof that the shogun's spies had gotten inside the palace.

But provoking Kihachi further probably wasn't the best strategy.

Jinnai nodded politely and went back into the building.

When all the bouts for the day were over and Jinnai and Sashichi left the castle to head for home, it was dark outside.

Two of Utsuki's five contenders had remained in the bracket. If they could win their bouts tomorrow and then again the next day, they would make it into the final ten and fight before the shogun himself. Sashichi only hoped that they would not have to face Hawk and Plum.

Back at the Kugimiya residence, Jinnai dragged himself into the workshop to resume his repairs on the golden macaw. But, unable to concentrate, he rose from his seat again less than an hour later.

By night, Eve rested in the basement room in this building

that Kyuzo used as his private work space. Jinnai felt uneasy about entering the room uninvited, but he had done so on several occasions when Kyuzo had been out. Guilt aside, for a former spy getting inside was no challenge at all.

He lifted a certain floorboard to reveal a steep, straight staircase. At the bottom of the staircase, cool and quiet, was the basement. It was roomier here than upstairs. Kyuzo sometimes spent days down here, lost in his work.

Moving into the depths, Jinnai slid a lacquered door aside. In the room beyond lay Eve.

Once a month, Kyuzo detached her head and limbs from her torso for a detailed inspection, placing each component on its own bench or platform. But tonight she was in one piece, lying utterly still on the central bench in her thin sleepwear. Her eyes were closed.

Jinnai walked to the bench and gazed down at her face. Something about her expression gave the illusion of deep, regular breathing. Her eyelashes were long and her lips only faintly colored, like a bud waiting to blossom.

As if drawn by some invisible force, Jinnai's hand reached slowly toward her breast.

Right on the verge of making contact, he came to his senses.

He shook his head.

Eve lay still as if nothing had happened.

I don't understand it.

Standing beside the Sacred Vessel on its bench, Kyuzo wiped the perspiration from his forehead with the back of his hand.

He had replaced every component that might have degraded over time, whether it appeared to have actually degraded or not.

The Vessel's construction was nearly identical to Eve's. Which meant that Kyuzo had every one of its millions of components in his head, down to the tiniest gear.

He knew that if a single gear-tooth length or the distance between two sesame-seed-sized cogs was off by the tiniest fraction, the mechanism would fail. But even after examining each one individually through the magnifying glass, Kyuzo had found no evidence of any mismatches.

If this were Eve's body, it would be running smoothly.

The more he'd seen of the Vessel's construction, the more firmly he had come to believe that Keian Higa had used his inspection of it as a pretext for recording its design and building a reproduction.

Namely, Eve.

Kyuzo pressed his fingertips into his eyelids and shook his head.

Having barely slept in days, he was near mental and physical exhaustion. Perhaps there was some subtle difference between Eve and the Vessel that he had failed to notice.

Several of the components in Eve's body were made of unknown alloys or other materials whose provenance was obscure. In the Vessel, different materials had been used for the corresponding parts, although they did weigh exactly the same.

Still seated, Kyuzo surveyed the Vessel. Its limbs were still detached, and its head was on a raised platform as if to look down on its own torso.

He had been so engrossed in examining its workings through the scope, he realized, that he had not considered it as a whole in some time.

Its eyes were closed as if asleep. The swellings on its chest retained their form despite the Vessel's prone position lying on its back, and the nipples at their peaks were pink like flower buds.

He felt a sudden urge to touch them and began to reach out before a wave of déjà vu struck him.

This had all happened before. Long before, when he was still a young man, learning his trade at Keian Higa's Institute of Machinery.

Just after his first meeting with Eve.

He closed his eyes and thought back on that day.

IV

Kyuzo stared at the hand he had just pulled back, then looked down at the half-built automaton on the platform.

Its head and torso were complete down to about the solar plexus, and half of its right arm was present. The rest was yet to be built.

When Kyuzo had first stolen into the workshop while Keian was away, he had mistaken it at first for the remains of a girl who had been carved up alive, and he had fallen over in terror.

But even in its partially complete state, on closer examination there could be no mistake: this was an automaton made in the form of a young woman.

On that first occasion, Kyuzo had wondered, horrified, if Keian Higa's soul had been captured by some malevolent spirit.

Did he intend to create a working replica of the human soul?

He had discussed the question of the soul with Keian often,

and the older man's thoughts were clear.

In the end, a human being is nothing but a fiendishly complex machine. There is no border between the soul and what is not the soul—only differences in complexity and diversity.

This was the position of that small, agreeable man, always full of smiles and surrounded by students.

Kyuzo wanted to argue, but he had no reply. He made his living building and repairing dolls for karakuri shows and great works like the eternal clock. He had some confidence in his abilities, but he realized then that he had never thought about these matters before.

The name of the Institute of Machinery was known even in Tempu, but Kyuzo had never imagined how advanced Keian's work truly was. In his conceited ignorance, he had agreed to the master of the Conch and Taiko's proposal that he enter the institute as a mole, thinking that he could at least steal a design or two.

Kyuzo gazed at Keian's half-built automaton and sighed.

It was beautiful despite the absence of life—or was it that absence that made it beautiful? An ageless beauty, unchanging, inviolable.

Worried that if he stayed too long the other students might notice, Kyuzo decided to leave.

"I'll be back, Eve," he said to the automaton.

He knew there would be no answer. He felt foolish even saying it, but there was something about the automaton that made him do so anyway.

He had named it "Eve" himself. It was the name of the courtesan said to live on the highest level of the Thirteen Floors in Tempu.

In truth, there was no such woman. The thirteenth floor was unoccupied, and the highest rank was left empty to prevent arguments among the women who were at the rank below. All this was well-known to the residents of the pleasure quarters and their savvier regulars, who treated the fictional Eve as a sort of guardian bodhisattva of the Thirteen Floors.

When Kyuzo had lived in Tempu, he had been credulous enough to long to see this Eve at least once before he died, until an acquaintance and habitual customer at the Thirteen Floors told him the truth.

The name of a woman who did not exist. It seemed ideal for the woman before him, who existed but had no life.

Kyuzo stepped out of Keian's private workshop, which stood apart from the main residence in a separate building surrounded by bamboo grass. He trod the narrow path through the grove and pushed open the gate in the hedge. Then he returned to his room in a corner of the main building and prepared to go out.

He had to meet Matsukichi.

The thought made his stomach ache.

The knowledge of his wrongdoing in betraying his master Keian and fellow students grew larger every day.

If Kyuzo had not been sent into the institute as a mole by Matsukichi, a spy with the shogun's intelligence service, he might never have become a student of Keian's at all.

But if it had not been his fate to meet Keian under different circumstances and become his student honestly, better to have never met him at all and lived out his life as just another karakuri artisan. Fortune could be cruel.

Matsukichi insisted that he report everything he saw at the

institute, hiding nothing. He seemed particularly interested in notes or diagrams related to the Sacred Vessel from the Age of Myth, which Keian was reportedly inspecting in the imperial palace, but Kyuzo had seen nothing of that nature.

Kyuzo had not told Matsukichi about Eve and did not intend to. She had no connection to the palace's secrets, as far as he could tell, and above all he could not bear the thought of her attracting interest from the wrong people and being exposed to danger.

"You haven't switched sides on me, have you?"

Matsukichi sat across from Kyuzo in a roadside establishment on the Hase Highway, not far from Utsuki Castle. The din coming through the floor betrayed the gambling tables downstairs. Secret talks were better held in busy, noisy places than quiet, isolated ones.

This meeting place would also allow Kyuzo to use gambling as an excuse should anyone become suspicious of his excursions and follow him here, although no one had so far. "Admitting" to gambling would also explain why he had kept his visits here secret.

"I don't know what you want me to tell you," Kyuzo said. "There is no suspicious activity within the Institute of Machinery, and none of the students have heard anything about his inspections of the Sacred Vessel at the palace." None of this was a lie, allowing Kyuzo to speak with genuine conviction.

"So you say. All right, then. I see you're in typically good humor, in any case." Matsukichi slurped at the sake in his cup and grimaced. "Even with the drink, these meetings of ours are no fun at all."

I couldn't agree more, Kyuzo thought.

"By the way, any news about the empress's condition? Since Keian's a regular palace visitor these days."

Kyuzo shook his head.

The empress was currently pregnant with her second child. Her firstborn had been a boy named Hiruhiko, so the imperial household was naturally hoping for a girl this time who could inherit the throne.

Physically, the empress was frail. Giving birth to Prince Hiruhiko had weakened her severely, and rumors had spread that he might be her last child.

So the shogun was interested in palace affairs too, Kyuzo mused. He had heard that the shogunate had been the main funder of the most recent relocation of the palace itself. The warrior clans were undeniably in the superior position today, but even they could not simply ignore the authority of the imperial household, which dated back to the Age of Myth.

The shogunate might have adopted the custom of cricket fighting and many other trappings of nobility, but to the imperial household it was still a shedder of blood, barred absolutely from even the outer rooms of the palace. The shogun appeared to be planning to marry his daughter into the imperial line, however, and if the empress had another son, the palace's utter dependence on the shogun would make it difficult to refuse his proposal.

Kyuzo assumed that Matsukichi was doing the bidding of some highly placed figure in the shogun's bureaucracy, but he did not know who that was. In truth, he had no idea what Matsukichi was scheming, or to what end.

A month or so later, Kyuzo was summoned to speak with Keian. The first words out of the older man's mouth were shocking.

"Her Majesty did not survive the delivery," said Keian.

Kyuzo was shocked. "And the heir?" he asked.

"Claimed by the gods."

So the child had died too.

"Naturally, this is not to be shared with anyone," Keian said.

Kyuzo reeled. Why would Keian share this momentous secret with the likes of him?

"The palace has decided to keep the news to themselves for now."

"It does not seem the sort of thing that can be kept hidden for long."

Keian nodded, a serious expression on his face. "It has been decided that I will build an automaton in the shape of a human," he said.

Kyuzo swallowed.

Notwithstanding the half-built automaton in Keian's workshop, the idea seemed reckless beyond belief.

"I find it hard to believe that it will fool anyone," Kyuzo said, "no matter how closely it resembles the empress."

"Not the empress, you fool," said Keian. "It will be in the image of the stillborn child."

Kyuzo mopped the sweat beading on his brow.

"The death of the empress will be reported when the time is right. Succession will pass to the infant, and a regent will be installed. I imagine that eventually Prince Hiruhiko will play that role."

To build an automaton in the form of an adult woman would be a staggering undertaking. But a baby could not speak and had little opportunity, except through cries, to convey its will to others. It seemed to Kyuzo that perhaps—just perhaps—what Keian proposed might be possible.

It must have been because he had seen Eve that it seemed this way to him. Certainly he would never have imagined such an automaton to be possible otherwise.

"The first step is to make an infant," Keian said. "As it develops, its components can be replaced one by one, bringing it closer to humanity in its gestures and behavior."

Much easier to start with a simple baby and gradually refine its functionality as it approached adulthood than to aim for perfection from the outset.

Of course, even Kyuzo's plan seemed just barely within the realm of possibility. But Kyuzo felt quiet excitement stir within him, and his hands trembled slightly.

"The other students at the institute are still learning and can be of no use to me when action is required immediately. But you were a karakuri artisan in Tempu. You have skills they do not. Will you help me?"

Kyuzo was startled but proud to learn that Keian saw that potential in him.

From that day on, whenever he had the chance, he visited

the execution grounds and dissected the bodies of pregnant women, newborn infants, and young children in particular, inspecting their insides closely.

Based on diagrams that Keian drew, Kyuzo carved a skeleton out of silver. Keian built a mechanism of gears and springs and clockwork to set inside it. Kyuzo set precious stones in milky-white glass to create eyeballs, and Keian created the workings that would control the expressions and movements of the face, cramming them inside the skull with no room to spare.

The two of them were possessed by a blasphemous drive to create life from the lifeless.

They threw themselves into the project, heedless of the passing time. After weeks of work, their automaton began to look increasingly like a baby.

As he honed their design, a thought came to Kyuzo.

A pregnant woman's body was home to not one soul but two.

On reflection, that was an extraordinary thing.

Where did the life in her womb come from, and when?

If souls came from elsewhere to reside in the human body, was it not possible that one might take up residence in the infant automaton they were building?

After a hundred days or more of work, the automaton's form, at least, was nearing completion.

Keian had been forced by unavoidable business to go out that evening. Mentally and physically exhausted, Kyuzo found himself unable to resist stealing into Keian's workshop for another look at Eve.

Entering the workshop in the bamboo grass grove, he found her lying faceup on her workbench, as usual. More parts had been added since he'd seen her last, and she was now complete to her elbows and knees.

Sitting beside her, Kyuzo gazed intently at her face. Her eyes were closed.

Her missing extremities gave her a certain ghoulish air, but unlike the corpses Kyuzo was by now thoroughly sick of seeing at the execution grounds, she had the color of radiant health, with a hint of red in her cheeks. It might have been his imagination, but she also seemed to have the faint fragrance of flowers.

"Eve," he said quietly.

Perhaps it was because he was tired. If not, perhaps because he was overworked and his feelings for this automata were even stronger than usual.

Until that night, he had sat gazing at her at length, but he had never touched her.

Because if a man such as he touched her, wouldn't she be polluted? Would this not destroy something pure? So it had always seemed to him.

He felt his heart pounding.

He reached toward her white chest.

The tip of his middle finger brushed against her nipple.

Hesitation. Then he softly placed his palm over her left breast.

Supple elasticity. Softness. Vulnerability.

He had the illusion of feeling his heartbeat traveling down his arm and through his fingertips into the automaton's heart.

Through her breast, mingled with his own pulse, Kyuzo felt a balance wheel within her rotate backward and strike a pendulum. A rhythmic, regular cycle began.

Her eyelids opened.

"Kyuzo...Kugimiya?" she said, quietly but distinctly.

Kyuzo leapt back from the bench, his whole body shaking.

Even while working with Keian on the infant automaton, some part of Kyuzo had viewed the project with skepticism, dismissing the possibility that an automaton might move or talk like a human, much less think like one.

Without rising from the workbench, Eve turned her head to look at him.

Even this was too much for him. Kyuzo fled the room.

V

"I never even imagined…"

As Eve finished her story, Jinnai could not help but exclaim in wonder. The Kyuzo he knew almost never let emotions show. To think that he had once acted this way!

The two of them were sitting together on the verandah behind the Kugimiya residence. Between them was the four-legged box with Eve's painting of a fin whale on it and something that had once been a man shut up inside.

"It was some time after that that Kyuzo closed his heart for good," she said.

"The foiled rebellion?" asked Jinnai.

Eve nodded, striking the box. She liked to carry it outside on days like this when the weather was fine, to sit in the sun. Kyuzo's students would see her chatting to it and cock their heads, remarking that she was a fine girl but did have a strange side to her. And every new student who joined the school, without fail, made the embarrassing mistake of sitting on it before being dressed down by Eve, her face red with fury.

Jinnai put a hand to his chin and thought.

Keian Higa's Institute of Machinery had taken in not just trained artisans like Kyuzo but also second and third sons from minor domains, as well as penniless ronin and the like. It had been a difficult time for the shogun's authority, and domains were seeing their holdings reduced or even dissolved entirely for the slightest offenses. Many of the dissatisfied and disgruntled had gathered under Keian.

Keian had only been a karakuri artisan himself, but he had received an unprecedented offer from the shogunate to be granted samurai rank and to head the refinery. Nevertheless, he had steadfastly refused this, and his connections with the imperial palace had been deep. This was what had secured for him the support of officials and country samurai from the smaller domains, who were worried what the shogunate might do next, as well as ronin with no hope of reentering official service.

Jinnai suspected that Keian's personal animus against the shogun had been slight. His main concern had likely been the prospect of the shogun gaining enough power to uncover the empress's secret and disturb the imperial tomb.

Put another way, it was a kind of parental feeling for the imperial automaton. Jinnai could not see it any other way: Keian's motivation had been to protect his daughter from the gawking eyes and filthy hands of those he feared would violate her.

When the previous shogun had died of illness and the

empress had formally ordered the currently reigning shogun, who was just eleven years old at the time, to take his place, Keian had finally begun to take concrete action. He used his skill with machinery to create short firearms that could be hidden in the front fold of a kimono and fired without flame. He made clockwork arson devices and automata that looked like birds or cats but were packed with explosives. All of these were part of his plan for the rebellion.

First, the ronin would rise in Tempu, lighting fires in a dozen or so strategic locations to start a raging inferno across the city. Next, men hidden around the magistrate's offices and Tempu Castle would take advantage of the confusion to assassinate as many high-placed officials as they could get their hands on.

Meanwhile, Keian would enter the imperial palace and wait for the report from his students before accepting the empress's orders to subjugate the shogun and having those orders promulgated across the land.

The automated empress was like a daughter to Keian, and he expected that many of his students' domains would willingly raise their banners and join the fight against the shogun, now the empress's enemy, alongside the ronin waiting in Tempu and Kamigata.

But all this planning had been for nothing. The mole planted in the institute by the shogun's intelligence service had seen to that.

And that mole was Kyuzo Kugimiya.

"I know you are a mole, Kyuzo," said Keian.

Kyuzo, summoned into the depths of the main house to meet with his master, was stunned. Still kneeling, he felt cold sweat trickle down his neck and into his armpits as the fists on his thighs trembled.

"How long have you...?"

"I have had my suspicions for some time. You meet with some kind of go-between for the shogun's spies in a gambling house, if I am not mistaken."

Matsukichi. If Keian knew that much, Kyuzo had no hope of talking his way free.

Keian stared at Kyuzo through half-closed eyes, as if seeing directly into his mind. His usual persona of the jovial old man was nowhere to be seen. Kyuzo could not meet his eyes.

Suddenly, a screen slid to the side.

Kyuzo tensed, thinking that one of Keian's ronin students had come to dispatch him with a sword.

But beyond the door stood a young woman.

She wore a vivid red kosode, and her black hair was twisted around a long *kanzashi*.

For a moment, Kyuzo did not recognize her. But then he knew who she was, and all words failed him as he cried out.

It was Eve.

Kyuzo stared as she took her place beside Keian, holding the front of her kosode in place as she sat down smoothly. She then made a formal bow to Kyuzo.

"I am Eve," she said.

When she looked up again, she had a faint smile on her face. Kyuzo could see his flustered form reflected in her sparkling eyes of dark agate.

"She is familiar to you, I think. As is her name."

Overwhelmed, Kyuzo could not answer.

"I understand that you stole into my workshop many times when I was away. Eve told me everything."

"I..."

He had thought the day when Eve woke and spoke to him had just been a dream or a fantasy arising from the shame he felt at what he was doing.

"But I do have one question. How did you set this automaton in motion?"

"How... ?" Kyuzo's voice cracked partway through the word. He was not sure what the other man meant.

"In theory, her mechanism was fine," Keian said, "but I simply could not get her to walk. But after contact with you, she began to move of her own will. So I ask again, *how*? What did you do?" By the end of his speech, Keian's brow was deeply furrowed, his voice urgent and low.

"I do not know."

Kyuzo searched his memory, but nothing in particular suggested itself.

"Fine," Keian said. "I understand that you gave her the name Eve as well. She insists on retaining it now."

Kyuzo's face burned. Under Keian's grilling, he realized for the first time that he had invested more in this lifeless automaton than he had in any living woman.

"I have used Eve's body as the basis for improving the imperial automaton," Keian said. "In sophistication it is now Eve's equal."

Kyuzo raised his head.

After they had completed the infant automaton—really more of an experiment—he had only been asked to make individual components based on provided schematics. He had never seen the upgraded automaton itself, since Keian's students were not permitted to accompany him into the palace.

The public, at least, believed that although the empress had passed on, her daughter and heir had survived and would one day inherit the reins of power from her older brother.

"To be honest," Keian said, holding Kyuzo's gaze. "I regret what you have become. My other students know nothing but theory, but in your hands lives the art and spirit of the machine— of its creation. This is a rare thing. Knowledge lies, but art does not. Understand this: divinity resides in the hands."

Keian was already well outside the bounds of their usual master-and-apprentice conversations.

"The gears and springs and other components your hands bring forth are free from error, whether of dimension or detail. They are also free from lies. That is why I decided to trust you."

"Master Keian..."

His voice but a hoarse whisper, Kyuzo trailed off, lost for words. Tears welled at the corners of his eyes.

"You were sent to the institute as a mole. It would be pointless to criticize you for the events that brought us together. In any case, you have been here ten years now. In your heart, I believe that you are on my side and that of the institute, not the shogun."

Kyuzo nodded, firmly, repeatedly. He would have supplemented this with words, but none came. He felt as if any reply he made here would only sound false.

"I assume you remain in contact with a go-between for the shogun. The truth is, that serves my purposes well."

Kyuzo gasped, realizing what Keian was working up to.

"The day of rebellion against the shogun is already set. The planning is underway."

Kyuzo had suspected as much. More people were coming and going than before, and many of them were clearly not there for lessons in karakuri design. Whether to report this to Matsukichi had kept him awake many nights of late.

"The rebellion begins on the first Day of the Hare in the twelfth month, at sunset—the Hour of the Rooster. Make sure your contact gets the message."

Kyuzo nodded, understanding his role: to pass false information to the shogunate so that they would be surprised when Keian made his move earlier.

What must be done must be done. If deceiving Matsukichi was the goal, he would simply report what Keian had said without mentioning that it was untrue.

He understood, too, that this was a test. Keian could have simply given him the false information without revealing what he knew. But he had chosen not to.

If he passed this test, Kyuzo thought, and endured what was to come, then he could finally be Keian's apprentice in full, with no secrets between them.

After leaving the room and making his preparations, Kyuzo set off for the inn. By coincidence, a meeting at the gambling house was already planned for that day. Matsukichi seemed suspicious about movements within the institute of late and demanded that Kyuzo see him more frequently than ever.

Matsukichi's company was never pleasant, but today Kyuzo's feet felt light as he walked toward his destination. He even felt a twinge of excitement at the prospect of deceiving the man.

If the plot against the shogun succeeded, Kyuzo would finally be free of Matsukichi and the intelligence service behind him.

Reaching the gambling house, he lowered the guard over his inner thoughts and headed for the second floor where Matsukichi was waiting.

Against his expectations, Matsukichi did not raise an eyebrow at Kyuzo's story. Instead, he scratched his chin with his fingertips and said, "The question is, who to believe?"

"What do you mean?" Kyuzo asked, feigning calm.

"The thing is, Kyuzo, what you've just told me doesn't match what my other source said."

Dread welled within Kyuzo. "Surely you don't..."

"If you thought you were the only mole there, think again," Matsukichi said, sipping from his cup. "Our other guy's one of the ronin that drop in there. I have contacts with Muta domain, and I've arranged for him to step into a nice official position there once everything's over."

Matsukichi grinned and threw back the rest of his cup.

"I guess Keian and his people have you figured out."

"That's..." Not knowing how to respond, Kyuzo fell silent.

"Fed you fake plans, a fake date. They know you're connected to the shogunate, and they think they can use you to put us off guard. But my other guy gave me a date ten days earlier. I'd say that's the real one, wouldn't you?"

Matsukichi nodded as if convinced by his own reasoning.

"You can't go back to the institute now. You know that, right? You've outlived your usefulness to them. Luckily, you still have me. We can head back to Tempu together in the morning."

"I..."

Matsukichi glowered at him. "I'm doing this for you, Kyuzo. Unless it interferes with some other plans you have, of course."

Kyuzo held his tongue. If Matsukichi realized that Kyuzo was in on the attempted deceit, he would be cut down right in the gambling house without hope of mercy. And that would also end his dream of becoming a true apprentice of Keian.

"I didn't send you into that place just to spy," Matsukichi continued. "The shogunate needs someone with your skills who's willing to put them to work for the world—unlike Keian, who keeps turning us down. Plus—"

Matsukichi's pupils suddenly seemed to expand.

"If those fools really do launch a rebellion against the shogun, everyone in the institute will be put away. You'll be the sole heir to the technology. Not a bad setup. You'll be made a samurai, with an official post and everything."

"You can't be serious."

Kyuzo had never dreamt of receiving such an unprecedented offer. No—not unprecedented. This was surely the same proposal that Keian had rejected. The shogun had given up on Keian and now hoped to bring Kyuzo to heel by dangling the same conditions.

"Oh, I'm very serious. I'll introduce you to my boss as soon as we get back to Tempu."

"I have no interest in meeting the head of the shogun's spies."

"I'm not talking about Kihachi. I mean someone much higher up. Likes to blow his own horn—or conch, if you get my drift."

Matsukichi's laugh was one of genuine amusement, although Kyuzo could not see why.

In any case, things were moving quickly in a direction he had not anticipated. Matsukichi was a boor, but he was not with the intelligence service for nothing. Catching him off guard and slipping away to return to the institute would be difficult and would definitely arouse his suspicion.

Kyuzo bit his lip hard. He cursed his own cowardice. Even at this stage, he still feared death, which left him no choice but to obey Matsukichi.

And so, on the eleventh month of the seventh year of the Shuyu era, magistrates from both the east and the west moved to arrest vast numbers of students and ronin from the Institute of Machinery. Many were caught red-handed with clockwork arson devices, ready to burn down half of Tempu.

Keian himself fled his residence just before the authorities reached it and took refuge in the imperial palace. After more than twenty days of steadily increasing pressure from the shogunate, however, the palace finally handed him over.

The planned imperial commission to subjugate the shogun, of course, was not forthcoming. The armies of the shogunate had camped around the palace in rings ten or twenty layers deep. The threat of war on the imperial household itself was obvious.

When Keian opened the palace gates to this ominous sight, his face was surprisingly calm, as if he had achieved some goal and made peace with his situation. He accepted his bonds without resistance.

Students and even regular visitors to the institute, as well as domain samurai and ronin with no connection to the rebellion itself, were tracked down and captured one by one. Several minor domains were completely dissolved, with the attempted rebellion cited as the cause.

At the execution grounds in Mitsutsujigahara, the Field of the Triple Crossroads, more than a hundred men were beheaded for involvement in the incident. The heads of Keian Higa and those deemed chief conspirators were left on display until the crows and maggots had stripped them of every shred of meat and they were sun-bleached skulls with only their hair remaining.

The declaration to the magistrates about the plot by Keian Higa and his associates contained two names. The first was a ronin who would later be restored to samurai status by the Muta domain.

The other was Kyuzo Kugimiya—"assistant at the shogunal refinery."

I died inside that day.

As Kyuzo looked down on the Vessel, which still showed no sign of motion, remorse washed over him.

Granted a sprawling property on the outskirts of the city, better paid by far as an "assistant" than the actual head of the refinery, he had brazenly, shamelessly survived to this day.

To destroy the other former mole at the institute and the entire domain that had taken him in, Kyuzo had planted an automated cricket on him at the tournament. Then he had used

Jinnai, working for the master of accounts, to seal Matsukichi's fate. Lord Haga, the man who had pulled the strings during the incident involving the imperial automaton, had been tricked into a course of action that ended in his domain's dissolution and his own suicide by shogunal decree.

In this way, Kyuzo had taken his revenge. But the dark mist that filled his heart had yet to clear.

After Keian had been beheaded and his head put on display, Kyuzo had been summoned to the refinery's workshop to inspect the machinery and papers confiscated from the institute. He had concealed the schematics for the imperial automaton by renaming the book *The Mechanism's Workings Are Obscure* and hiding it in plain sight among the other volumes.

But as he examined the confiscated goods, Kyuzo noticed something peculiar: the automaton who called herself Eve was not among them.

He checked the register of executions and imprisonments but found no record of a young woman who might have been her. In any case, if she had been captured and revealed to be a human-scale automaton, there would have been uproar. Only a handful of people even knew of the existence of automata like this, who moved and spoke as people did.

In his role as refinery assistant, Kyuzo himself had never let the secret slip. He doubted that he would have been believed anyway, without Eve herself as proof.

Then came a humid day of early-summer rains.

As hollow inside as ever, Kyuzo was reading alone in the house the shogunate had given him when he noticed that a visitor was at his gate.

He opened the front door. It was noon, but the sky was cloudy and the day dark. The red kosode of the woman at his gate seemed to bleed vividly into the gray that surrounded her.

She held her umbrella low, concealing everything but the lower half of her face.

Her red lips were curved into a smile.

Eve.

Heedless of the rain, Kyuzo was rooted to the spot as she shuffled toward him.

"I've been looking for you, Kyuzo Kugimiya."

She raised her umbrella, revealing gleaming, agate-green eyes that pierced his own with their gaze.

From this distance, he could see that the hem of her kosode was dirtied and torn. She wore no footwear save *tabi* socks so tattered they were little more than scraps of fabric. He felt the length of her journey keenly.

"My body requires your assistance in many places."

Kyuzo fell to his knees where he stood, muddying his clothing in a puddle. He collapsed forward and pressed his forehead against the paving stones, as if drinking the muddy water. Then he began to weep.

They were the first tears he had shed since Keian's death.

And that was the last time he ever revealed any sort of emotion before Eve.

As he gazed at the Vessel on its bench now, something like those long-lost emotions welled up within him once more.

He yearned to reach out and touch it.

Of course, as part of his inspection, he had poked and prodded it everywhere, but this was different. He wanted to touch the sleeping Vessel not as a maker of automata but as a man.

A memory came to him of Eve, lying in Keian's workshop still incomplete.

He felt his heart pound.

He reached out toward the Vessel's pale chest and slipped his hand between the folds of its white silk underrobe.

How long had it been since he'd last felt this way?

He felt a pang of melancholy at his advancing years beside Eve, still young and beautiful, and now the Vessel that was her twin.

Gently, he cupped the Vessel's left breast in the palm of his hand.

Supple elasticity. Softness. Vulnerability.

Kyuzo was overcome not by lust but by nostalgia. Longing for what was now lost.

Yes. What Eve had once meant to him—

Suddenly he felt movement through his palm.

For an instant, he wasn't sure if it was the beating of his own heart or the workings of the equivalent mechanism inside the Vessel.

He looked down to see the Vessel's long-lashed eyes slowly open.

Next, like a flower bud blooming, her pale pink lips parted. White teeth carved of pearl oyster shell gleamed between them.

"Kyuzo...Kugimiya?"

The illusion was complete. For Kyuzo, time had run backward to Eve's awakening.

VI

The great hall in the castle keep had been furnished with a long, carpeted bench on which sat a row of insect habitats of various shapes and sizes.

These were the crickets that had lost their bouts and would not be competing before the shogun. Crickets could not survive the winter; this was the only season they would see. They had been reared solely to fight for the shogun's amusement, so after the tournament they were presented to him as gifts.

Dominating the room was a large five-sided table of ebony. This was where the fights would take place. The finest seat at the table was for the shogun. Two more sides were reserved for the referee and the official. The final two were for the trainers of the west and east corner for each bout. Behind the trainers stood two more carpeted benches, each holding five habitats—

one cricket for each side of the five bouts to take place in the shogun's presence.

A number of nervous-looking men were sitting near the table on the east side, and one of them was Sashichi. One of Utsuki's crickets had made it through to the tournament's final round, giving Sashichi his first opportunity to wield the senso in the shogun's presence.

Opposite Sashichi on the west side was a trainer who was a cricket-fighting official himself. Hawk and Plum, the shogun's cricket, was also among the final ten.

Another several dozen men from various domains sat some distance from the ebony table, waiting impatiently for the shogun to arrive.

Only those who were at the table itself looking into the fighting basin could follow the bout directly, but this was well understood by all. The referee's wooden fan told the story for those who could not see. His grip, the angle at which he held it, how he moved it—all of this conveyed information about the progress of the fight in a code that every enthusiast knew.

Those close to the table had been waiting quietly at first, but now they began to murmur to each other uneasily. It had already been an hour since the appointed start time.

Jinnai, too, had the vague feeling that something had gone awry.

The first clue was when Kihachi Umekawa, who had positioned himself in a corner of the great hall to watch Jinnai, had disappeared.

Something that required Kihachi's presence despite his having other plans was clearly not a minor issue.

As Jinnai was mulling this over, the six-paneled set of sliding paper screens at the back of the hall, painted with a bamboo thicket and a tiger, slid open from the middle.

The whole room froze, thinking that the shogun had arrived. A moment later, the tension in the assembled faces was replaced by confusion.

Standing in the opening between the screens was a woman dressed only in a thin underrobe.

"Where is he?" she asked, scanning the room with a look of concern. Her words did not seem to be addressed to anyone in particular. She looked right through those present, as if the great hall were empty.

The most noticeable detail, however, was that she was spattered head to toe with blood.

Eve?!

Jinnai, among the crowd assembled for the tournament, was about to call out to her when he stopped himself.

No. That wasn't Eve.

Which meant it was—

Jinnai rose to his feet, but before he could move forward, the official who had been sitting at the table approached the woman.

"Do you realize where you are, woman?" he demanded. "How did you get in here?" His hand was on the hilt of his sword, but to Jinnai he looked more unsettled than angry.

"Are you of the shogunate?" she asked.

"I am. As an official at this tourna—" His words became a scream.

Jinnai did not have a clear view from where he stood, but he could see the woman's long, slender arm extended toward the official's face and the official scrabbling at it with his hands.

Finally the rest of the room saw what the woman was doing—plunging her thumb and index finger deep into the official's eyes.

The whole room snapped to attention, everyone half rising to their feet.

The woman stepped into the room, dragging the screaming, thrashing official behind her by the eye sockets. He left two red streaks of blood on the tatami mats behind him.

The referee and trainers who had been at the ebony table backed away hurriedly, faces white with terror. Sashichi scrambled toward Jinnai, practically on all fours.

"Jinnai! Is—is that—?"

"No," said Jinnai. "That isn't Eve." He seized Sashichi by the nape of the neck. "Listen to me! Leave the castle and go to the house. Tell Eve what has happened."

"What about you?"

"I'm going to look for Master Kyuzo. Whatever happens, don't do anything rash until I bring him out safely."

With that, Jinnai all but tossed Sashichi out of the room.

He looked back at the woman. Still dragging the now-limp official behind her, she was roaming the great hall craning her neck to peer this way and that, clearly searching for something. She did not seem to notice the tension and fear that now filled the room.

She moved just like Eve.

Noticing the insect habitats on the long carpeted bench by the wall, the woman cast the official's body aside and went to investigate.

One by one, she tore off the paper seals to see what was inside. Every time she did, a cricket would spring out of the habitat, and she would let out an incongruous "Oh!" of surprise.

Was this the Sacred Vessel from the Age of Myth?

No, Jinnai realized. This was the automaton that Keian Higa had built in imitation of the real Sacred Vessel. This was Eve.

"There she is!"

Before Jinnai had decided what to do, half a dozen grim-looking men dressed for battle—domain samurai, presumably—kicked in the sliding screen and poured into the hall. About the same number of men ran in through another entrance dressed in simple work clothes. These were the gardener agents of the shogun's intelligence service. Some of their faces were familiar to him.

About half of the people who had originally been in the great hall had already fled.

Swords drawn, the warriors and gardeners approached the Vessel from behind as she inspected the cricket habitats.

One of the men stepped forward and brought his blade down on her unprotected shoulder.

Instead of felling her in a gout of blood, the sword snapped and clattered onto the floor without harming her in any visible way.

The Sacred Vessel slowly turned.

There was no rage or hate in her face, but within moments she had grabbed the warrior by his topknot and thrown him into the air. He tumbled in an arc that brought him down headfirst on the carpeted bench. The bench cracked in two pieces, and the man's neck bent at an awful angle.

The cricket habitats that had been on the table scattered onto the floor. The ones she had not checked yet cracked open, allowing their inhabitants to escape across the tatami mats.

"Wait!" the Vessel said, panicking. "Stop!"

She hurried after the fleeing insects, leaving the broken-necked man to twitch behind her. The sight was almost comical.

As she tried to cup her hands over one of the crickets, looking on the verge of tears, one of the gardeners moved in and swung his sword at her. She caught the blade in her hand irritably, then pulled it out of the gardener's grasp and started to wave it around.

"Please don't tread on the crickets!" she cried, voice rising to an unhinged shriek as she wildly swung the blade. "Don't step on them!" Several men fell at her feet, already dead.

Making no attempt to parry or dodge the blows aimed at her, she moved forward in a straight line, slashing all who stood in her way so that even those with considerable skill were helpless against her. Even when a sword ran the Vessel through, it did not seem to hurt her or affect her, not even when blade struck bone and snapped off inside her.

The blood of the warriors who had opposed her spattered across the floor, the ceiling, the kicked-in sliding screens.

The gardeners had already vanished. *Must have recognized their disadvantage and gone to call for reinforcements*, Jinnai thought.

He realized with a start that he was the only man left in the room.

What's more, he was unarmed. Kihachi's suspicion that he was trying to smuggle something untoward into the castle had seen Jinnai thoroughly searched before he entered.

The Vessel came to a halt, sword dangling from one hand. She seemed to be at a loss. Then she looked at Jinnai.

The crimson smears of blood on her face only emphasized the fairness of her skin. Jinnai saw great beauty there.

"Are you of the shogunate?" she asked.

Jinnai shook his head. "No," he said.

"I see." Appearing to lose interest in him at once, the Vessel resumed her search, flipping over corpses to look under them.

Jinnai heard several dozen men in the corridor outside approaching at a run.

He hesitated, then decided to make himself scarce.

Finding Kyuzo and seeing him out to safety was a more pressing concern than the Vessel. He had an uneasy premonition that Kyuzo might already be in grave danger.

Running out into the corridor, he almost collided with a group of samurai and gardeners.

Kihachi was among them.

"This better not be your doing, Jinnai," he snarled.

"Shut up and listen," Jinnai said. He pointed at his chest. "I'm Jinnai Tasaka, apprentice of the great artisan Kyuzo Kugimiya. The woman in that hall right now is an automaton. Those dull blades won't even scratch her skin, let alone break her bones."

Some of the men in the group looked shocked.

Must have already seen a lot of their fellows die.

"If you want to stop her, aim for the solar plexus," Jinnai said, recalling a story Kyuzo had told him about another rogue automaton. "There's a place there where her skin was made thinner. Jab a finger in and push the mechanism behind her breastbone. Her clockwork will disengage and wind down, and she'll—"

"Don't listen to him!" Kihachi screamed. "He's a former agent of the Conch and Taiko. A traitor to the service!"

At this prompt, one of the warriors rushed toward Jinnai as he raised his sword.

Jinnai dove sideways through one of the doors in the corridor, smashing through it and rolling into the room beyond.

Half of the men in the corridor ran on to the great hall to subdue the Vessel. The rest poured into the room after Jinnai to finish him off.

"We don't have time for this now!" Jinnai cried, but the men around him were too ready to fight to listen.

If he let them surround him, that would be the end. Domain samurai aside, all of the familiar faces among the gardeners were better trained than him. Taking them on alone and unarmed would be suicide.

Kihachi stepped through the ring of men forming around Jinnai to stand before him. "I should have killed you when I had the chance," he said. "I've always been too sentimental for my own good." He accepted a sword from a nearby gardener and moved closer.

Jinnai dropped into a low stance and watched him closely.

"Goodbye, Jinnai."

Kihachi's blade began to fall.

Jinnai tensed in anticipation.

Then Kihachi's arm stopped, as if caught on something in midair.

A moment later, half the arm fell onto the ground like a sliced daikon.

For a moment, even Kihachi himself did not seem to follow what had happened.

Then he began scrabbling at his neck with his sole remaining hand as his body rose five inches off the ground.

Something had been pulled tight around his neck, sinking into the flesh just under his Adam's apple. Dark blood welled from the line for an instant. Then his body fell heavily to the ground, followed an instant later by his tumbling head.

Jinnai looked around in confusion. He saw something like glinting thread above him.

Then that glint sliced through the air. The men surrounding Jinnai fell like dominoes as their legs were severed beneath them.

Jinnai looked up. To prevent intruders hiding in the ceiling, it was open to the rafters. Fifteen or twenty feet above him, he saw a figure in indigo shinobi garb standing on a rafter.

"Long time no see, Jin."

The figure reeled in her wires and stored the weights at their ends in her sleeves, then somersaulted through the air to land before him, one knee on the floor.

"Kasuga?"

The last time he had seen the former palace ukami, she had been just a girl of fourteen or fifteen. Ten years later, she was more mature. She might even have been wearing makeup; in any case, her red lips gave her a stern, handsome look.

"What are you doing here?" Jinnai asked. It was too soon for Sashichi to have sent anyone.

"Eve told me I should drop by." Kasuga picked up the sword of the closest fallen warrior and tossed it to Jinnai. "Her Majesty and I went in for maintenance, but a couple of hours ago Eve started getting fidgety. A gut feeling, maybe."

"Eve?"

Kasuga nodded.

Had the awakening of the Vessel, her twin, caused some sympathetic resonance?

"She says Kyuzo's missing," Kasuga said.

"He has to be in the castle somewhere. And I think I know where."

Jinnai jammed the sword into the obi around his waist.

"Looks like you've found yourself some real trouble this time," said Kasuga. "When did you take up tinkering with karakuri, anyway? It doesn't suit you at all."

"Save it," Jinnai said, and broke into a run. Kasuga stayed right on his tail.

They left the main building, and Jinnai headed directly for the lower western courtyard.

On the way they passed many guards and domain samurai who had fled the great hall and were wandering around nervously, not sure what to do next. None paid any attention to Jinnai and Kasuga.

They cleared the green bamboo barrier in a single bound and kept going. In this part of the castle, they were alone.

Racing through the bleak, skeletal plum grove, they came to the area with the storehouses.

Jinnai had a hunch that one of them was being used as an impromptu workshop for Kyuzo's inspection of the Vessel. His plan had been to search them one by one, but he noticed immediately that one door was already ajar. Without hesitating, he ran through it.

In the dim room, he saw walls and shelves crammed with familiar tools and materials.

There was a workbench in the middle of the room, and beside

it was a slumped figure.

"Master Kyuzo!"

Jinnai ran to Kyuzo and crouched at his side.

Then came the horrific realization.

Both of Kyuzo's arms had been torn off at the shoulder, complete with the sleeves of his brown kosode. He looked like a doll mistreated by a violent child.

Aghast, Jinnai put his ear to Kyuzo's chest. His heartbeat was faint, but he was still breathing.

He had lost a terrible amount of blood, though. It had poured from his wounds to form a sticky, coagulating pool on the floor. His face was white, and when Jinnai helped him sit up straighter, his skin was cold.

"Is he dead?" asked Kasuga.

"No," Jinnai said after a long pause.

"He won't be repairing any more automata, though," she said with concern.

The hands that Kyuzo had used to craft automata of near-divine accomplishment were gone.

This could not be. It was precisely in those hands that Kyuzo's divinity resided.

"We have to take him home," said Jinnai. "He's still breathing." He hoisted Kyuzo over his shoulder. The old man groaned, although whether he was conscious was unclear.

"Did the Sacred Vessel do this?" asked Kasuga.

"So it would appear."

The Vessel must have attacked Kyuzo as soon as she awoke and then left him dying in the storehouse while she pursued her own ends.

Was she truly attacking as wildly and without distinction as it appeared? Or was there something deeper at work—some mechanism Keian Higa had built into her?

That would explain a lot. Keian had surely died convinced of Kyuzo's betrayal. If he had done some tinkering with the Vessel before leaving the palace to surrender...

No feats of deduction were necessary. The sealed-up Vessel had been wound for revenge on the shogunate, in anticipation of the moment when the shogun seized control of the palace and his agents opened the imperial tomb.

The trap might have been designed to spring into action the moment the iron cabinet was opened. But for whatever reason, at some point during its years underground, the Vessel had stopped working.

Until Kyuzo's inspection and repairs had revived her.

"What is Her Majesty going to do?" Kasuga fretted. She seemed more concerned about the survival of Kyuzo's skills than his physical form.

It made sense. To Kasuga, a life in service to the imperial automaton was a life well spent.

Kyuzo's life might be saved, but his work on automata was essentially over. Jinnai well understood Kasuga's concern about the empress. He was worried about Eve himself.

Kyuzo's arms were lying in the corner, but there was no point taking them home. They were of no use to anyone anymore.

Exiting the storehouse with Kasuga, Jinnai saw smoke rising from the castle keep.

"Kasuga," he said. "I need you to carry Master Kyuzo home. If a man named Sashichi turns up, tell him to get the word out to the other students—as of today, Kyuzo Kugimiya's school is closing its doors."

"What about you?"

"I'm going back to the keep."

"Why?" said Kasuga, shifting Kyuzo onto her own shoulders. "Let it burn."

Kasuga had once been a lady of the innermost sanctum. She had given up that life to free the imperial automaton, but she likely took a dim view of the shogun's intrusion into the palace. If the men of the shogunate were slaughtered en masse by the Vessel they had awakened, that was no concern of hers.

Kasuga was slightly surprised by how light Kyuzo was. It was due to the missing arms, no doubt.

"The Sacred Vessel is Eve's twin," said Jinnai. "I can't just leave her." He had no idea what he was actually going to do. All he knew was that the thought of her captured and helpless in the hands of the shogun's spies was unbearable.

"I understand," said Kasuga. She had thrown her life away for an automaton, too. Their circumstances were different, but she surely understood Jinnai's feelings for Eve—and, by extension, the Vessel—even if they could not be put into words.

Jinnai watched her run swiftly off, still carrying Kyuzo. Then he turned back toward the keep.

By now it was an inferno. Smoke and flames erupted from the windows and under the eaves.

Jinnai readjusted his sword and ran toward it.

As he approached the stone walls of the keep, the air shimmered with heat. Sparks showered down along with scorched and broken roof tiles.

He saw a warrior fleeing the scene and seized his arm.

"The woman! Where is she?" he demanded.

"S-still i-in the keep," stammered the man.

Jinnai nodded and let him go, then raced up the stone staircase and into the keep.

It felt deserted inside. By now everyone else must have fled.

The fire seemed to have started on an upper floor, because the lower floors were still only filled with thin smoke. Flames always sought to rise, so he probably had some time. But if one of the main pillars burned out, the whole upper section of the castle could crash down on him.

He ran first to the great hall where the final round of the cricket-fighting tournament was to have been held. The scene was very different now. Habitats and cages lay scattered across the floor, and here and there were smears where panicking men had trampled the same insects they had once so solicitously raised.

Jinnai headed deeper into the keep, kicking down screens and doors instead of wasting the time to open them properly.

He found a steep staircase leading upward and scaled it rapidly, cornering the tight turns at the landings.

The smoke was thicker on the floor above, but he still saw no flames.

Several corpses in battle gear lay around him. The Vessel's handiwork, he presumed.

As he searched for the stairs to the next floor up, he heard a beam crack.

"Sacred Vessel!" he called out desperately. "If you are here, show yourself!"

He had not expected it to work.

From outside he heard the sound and felt the shudder of eaves collapsing and a landslide of roof tiles clattering down the side of the building.

He found the next flight of stairs and had just stepped onto the first step when he saw the white feet of a woman descending the stairs from above.

Jinnai stopped and removed his sword, still in its scabbard, from his belt. Drawing the blade, he tossed the scabbard to one side. It could only get in the way.

Step-by-step, the feet descended the staircase.

The fire on the next floor up looked intense and was sending a constant spray of sparks and burning fragments into the staircase.

There was no telling when the whole keep might collapse. And yet the Vessel came slowly. Even irritatingly slowly.

When her lower half had come into view, he saw that she was carrying something.

A moment later he realized that it was a head.

The shogun's head.

By now the Vessel was almost fully in view.

Where is he?

Those had been her first words to the crowd in the great hall. Had she been looking for the shogun? And yet...

In her other hand the Vessel held a sword.

The flames had burned most of her hair off by now. The thin underrobe she wore had been reduced to rags by the sword blows she had endured, and now those rags were scorched as well.

She was a pitiful sight. In one place her skin was torn, revealing her gleaming metal rib cage and the endlessly whirling gears and clockwork within.

As she descended she swung the shogun's head like a watermelon from the market. If she felt any nervousness or excitement at having beheaded the shogun himself, she showed none.

Finally she noticed Jinnai and spoke.

"Are you of the shogunate?"

Jinnai braced himself for single combat and said, "I am."

It seemed clear by now that Keian Higa had designed her to kill not just the specific individuals against which he sought vengeance, but anyone who worked for the shogunate. And so she asked the same question of everyone she met and killed them if they answered in the affirmative. He felt a pang at her earnestness and immaturity.

But isn't this the natural state of the automaton? he thought as he raised his sword. As Kyuzo's apprentice, he had learned much about automaton construction but still harbored certain doubts.

Kyuzo argued that automata were soulless.

Eve, for example, might laugh as if happy and cry as if sad, but this was a masquerade orchestrated by gears and springs and clockwork and metal wires and quicksilver-filled tubes under her skin. The Eve that actually *felt* happy or sad did not exist.

Jinnai granted that Eve's workings contained no component that could control a soul.

But were humans any different?

Jinnai had accompanied Kyuzo to countless dissections at the execution grounds as part of his studies. Each one had deepened his conviction that Kyuzo was mistaken.

No matter how minutely you dissected the human body, you found nothing that embodied the soul or called up emotions and memories.

Where did the soul come from? Where, in the body or brain, did it conceal itself while a human still lived? These question had always bothered Jinnai.

If he had not met Eve, he doubted that he would ever have given such issues a thought.

And it was those feelings for Eve on Jinnai's part that gave Eve life.

Automata like Eve and the empress showed human behavior as a response to the care and love they received from humans. Their life was in that behavior.

The Vessel had lain in the imperial tomb since the Age of Gods, sealed away with full awareness. For a being with life, such loneliness would have been intolerable.

When had she finally become ensouled? *Probably*, Jinnai thought, *when Kyuzo named her.*

The replica of Eve that stood before him now had slept bearing within her Keian's enmity for the shogunate and all its works. Perhaps what had awoken her was Kyuzo's own self-loathing, his bitter regret.

Eve was bright and cheerful. Why not? Everyone loved Eve.

On the surface, this Vessel was Eve's twin. But no one had given her their heart.

"Poor thing," Jinnai said. The words came as a surprise even to himself.

But the Vessel was still approaching. And his answer to her question had changed her expression dramatically.

The only sure way to stop her was the method he had tried to share with Kihachi. He would have to punch through the hole in her solar plexus and disengage the mechanism behind her breastbone.

It was a close-range operation. She would have time to react. Was he willing to die to see this through?

Yes, he thought. *I am.*

Perhaps it was her resemblance to Eve that made him feel this way. If there was no one else to give the Vessel their heart, he would just have to do it himself. A double suicide for the sake of this lonely automaton who had slept so long in hell.

Jinnai adjusted his stance. He would knock her sword from her hand, throw away his own, and leap at her.

And then part of the ceiling fell.

Blackened beams and rafters crashed to the floor, still engulfed in flames. The sound was deafening.

The Vessel did not even glance at the vortex of fire behind her.

Jinnai stepped forward.

As he did, she threw the shogun's head into the flames and swung at him with her sword.

Blade clashed against blade.

Even with a two-handed grip, it took all of Jinnai's strength to withstand the force she brought to bear with a single arm.

As he struggled, her other hand reached for his neck.

Jinnai prepared himself for the end.

Then he heard a dry sound at his feet, like someone stepping on a bean.

"Oh!"

Letting her sword clatter to the floor, the Vessel looked down and raised her foot.

Jinnai looked down too.

Underneath her foot was a crushed cricket.

Jinnai recognized it immediately: it was Hawk and Plum, the cricket that Kihachi had captured at the palace. The cricket rumored to have come out of the imperial tomb.

The automated cricket that had been sealed in the tomb with her.

The Vessel wailed piteously and collapsed forward. Jinnai caught her, bracing himself against the weight.

He saw what had happened.

She had not been searching for the shogun. She had come in search of Hawk and Plum.

When Keian had closed her up in the tomb, this cricket had been with her. Why, Jinnai did not know. Perhaps the cricket was like Eve—a design from the Age of Myth, preserving the knowledge of the ancients in its very form.

But to the Vessel, it had been her only friend through years of darkness and solitude.

"Don't cry," Jinnai said. The Vessel clung to him, and he hugged her tightly.

Her tears dampened his shoulder.

He knew the design. Behind her eyes of agate and glass were two tear ducts made of specially tanned swim bladders that were found in fish. When her face contorted, a mechanism of springs and clockwork squeezed the ducts and the water inside them spilled out.

But what did that matter?

It was not clockwork that had brought these tears to her eyes. It was grief.

Jinnai moved his hand to her chest, extended a finger, and pushed it into her solar plexus.

The Vessel offered no resistance.

He pressed on the mechanism behind her breastbone, and her movements stopped.

As deadweight, the Vessel was too heavy for Jinnai to support. He lowered her to the floor.

From close up, it was clear that the crushed insect had indeed been an automaton too. Gears the size of sesame seeds and even tinier springs were scattered around its exoskeleton.

The Vessel's lashes and cheeks were still damp with tears. She looked as if she were sleeping.

The building lurched violently.

Jinnai left the Vessel where she was and backed away. He heard and felt a series of thuds above him, until a beam so gigantic he could hardly have gotten both arms around it pierced the ceiling and came crashing down almost vertically.

The Vessel and her cricket were engulfed in flames.

The skin that covered her body bubbled and melted, gradually revealing her carved skeleton and the mechanisms it contained.

Shaking off the urge to stay where he was and watch to the end, Jinnai forced himself to dive out of the nearest window, smashing the wooden lattice that covered it. He landed on the eaves and kept running, leaping free of the keep just as the mighty walls collapsed inward.

VII

Tempu Castle blazed like a torch held aloft above the city, visible from its every corner.

Crowds were already arriving to gape at the scene. Jinnai hurried through them and made his way back to the Kugimiya residence.

There was still work to be done.

"Master Kyuzo!"

Hearing only echoes in the main residence, he ran to the workshop in the yard. He opened both doors and hurried down the stairs to find everyone there before him.

"Jin!" Eve said. It was strange to see her after having left her identical twin in the burning castle only moments earlier.

Kasuga was in the corner, leaning against the wall with her arms crossed. She had changed from her indigo shinobi gear into a more subdued pink kosode.

On the central workbench lay the imperial automaton.

Her head and limbs had been removed and placed on their separate platforms, connected by their sagging bundles of steel and tubes.

"Who... ?" Jinnai asked.

"He told us to make sure you could start immediately," said Eve. Jinnai followed her gaze and saw Kyuzo. His shoulders had been bandaged, but blood was already beginning to seep through the white cloth.

Without opening his eyes, Kyuzo muttered, "You're late." His breathing was shallow. "But you did make it back before I died. Well done."

"Master Kyuzo—"

Kyuzo's eyes flew open. "Inspection and maintenance of the imperial automaton begins now."

"But in your condition—"

"As of now, Jinnai, this work falls to you. I will guide you through the key points of its construction—every secret it contains. But there isn't much time. This is your final lesson. Make sure it sticks."

"But..." Jinnai was aghast. Neither his knowledge nor his dexterity were anywhere near the level of Kyuzo's.

"Believe me," said Kyuzo, "I too would have preferred a worthier successor. But here we are. Stop arguing and do the work."

Jinnai looked at Kasuga. She nodded grimly.

It looked like he had no other choice.

He picked up the monocular scope from the table where the

tools were laid out. It was the one Kyuzo always used. Fitting it against his eye, he adjusted the dial with trembling hands to focus the lens.

The rest was a blur.

He did remember the things Kyuzo told him: how the imperial automaton was constructed, how to repair it, the secrets of manufacturing the necessary materials. All this stuck with him as if carved on his mind with hammer and chisel. But how he had managed to pull off those near-divine feats of workmanship and finish the work was a hazier matter—a shimmering memory glimpsed through mist.

According to Eve and Kasuga, he and Kyuzo had worked for three days and three nights straight, without food or rest.

Kyuzo cursed his clumsiness and slowness on the uptake. But ultimately the work was a success. The newly repaired automaton opened her eyes again. Kyuzo sighed as if in relief, and that was his last breath. Jinnai collapsed in exhaustion, Kyuzo's final words still with him.

The construction of Eve's body taught me everything Keian Higa knew. You must learn from her too.

"It's a bleak idea, growing older and older while Eve stays young forever," Jinnai said, sitting on the verandah beside Kasuga. "How does it make you feel?"

"Me?" Kasuga's eyes widened. She put her hand to her chin in thought. "Considering what it must feel like for Her Majesty to watch me grow old as she remains in her youthful form, I think I have the better side of it."

This answer startled Jinnai a little. "Outmatched again, I see," he said. Where he was uncertain and hesitant, Kasuga was remarkable clearheaded.

In Kyuzo's younger days, he had surely felt deeply for Eve. He had often claimed that automata had no emotions, no heart, but of late Jinnai had come to suspect that this was simply how Kyuzo had put an end to his own feelings. Still, what lay in the heart of another was as unknowable as the truth about whether automata had hearts at all.

Perhaps Kasuga had the unwavering confidence she did because she and the empress were servant and master rather than man and woman, which called for a different kind of dedication.

Certainly he had never considered the matters he agonized over from Eve's point of view.

That day, Jinnai, Kasuga, and the empress accompanied Eve to Nakasu Kannon.

The giant tent was back in the plaza beyond Bonten Gate for the first time in ten years. This had been the opportunity Kasuga and the empress had needed to visit Kyuzo's workshop.

Publicly, the shogun was said to have died in the fire. The new shogun had already been proclaimed—not exactly smoothly but with less turmoil than expected.

The keep of Tempu Castle no longer loomed above the city, and Jinnai hadn't heard of plans to build another.

Times had changed since the days of Keian Higa's plot. The shogunate's authority was as firm as bedrock, unshaken by the minor detail of the man at the top being replaced. Even if Tempu

Castle had no keep, the chances of war were slim. Whether that was good or bad, Jinnai could not say.

Kasuga and the empress walked hand in hand ahead of him. They had been the same age once; now, Kasuga looked like an indulgent older sister. The next time he met them, they might appear to be mother and child. Beyond that, grandmother and grandchild? In any case, this was surely what they wanted.

They parted with a promise to return when more repairs were needed, and Jinnai waited for Eve to complete her hundred prayers.

She still prayed to become human one day. As he moved the abacus for her, he prayed that one day he might be able to grant that wish.

Finally she was finished. "Shall we go?" he asked.

How long had Kyuzo's feelings for Eve lasted? Had those youthful passions smoldered within him to the very end?

Returning to the Kyuzo residence, Jinnai and Eve descended to the workshop basement and approached the table.

Eve smiled slightly, tilting her head. "No need for false modesty," she said. "Kyuzo told you to learn from my form."

Jinnai nodded and placed his hands on her collar to remove her clothing.

His heart was ringing like an alarm bell.

"Your hands are shaking," she said. A mischievous grin.

"Eve...I..." Jinnai felt unable to hide what he felt any longer.

But Eve interrupted him.

"One day, when you have the technique, I hope you will make a body for Tentoku," she said.

The shaking in his hands stopped.

Jinnai burst out laughing.

"Now I understand why Kyuzo never got around to that," he said.

And he also understood how Kyuzo had felt, to the very end.

Eve looked confused. "What do you mean?" she said.

"He was jealous. Of your feelings for that stool."

"Tentoku is not a stool!" Eve said, reddening in anger.

ROKURO INUI was born in 1971 in Tokyo. In 2010, he won the Konomys Award for *Kanzen Naru Kubinagaryu no Hi* (A Perfect Day for Plesiosaurs) and the Asahi Period Novel Prize for *Shinobi Gaiden* (Ninja Legend). His other books include *Oni to Mikazuki* (The Ogre and the Crescent Moon), the Takano Clinic series of mystery novels, and *Leipzig no Inu* (The Dog of Leipzig).

HAIKASORU
THE FUTURE IS JAPANESE

TRAVEL SPACE AND TIME WITH HAIKASORU!

A SMALL CHARRED FACE—KAZUKI SAKURABA

What are the "bamboo"?
They are from China.
They look just like us.
They live by night.
They drink human lifeblood but otherwise keep their distance.
And every century, they grow white blooming flowers.

A boy name Kyo is saved from the precipice of death by Bamboo, a vampire born of the tall grasses. They start an enjoyable yet strange shared life together, Kyo and the gentle Bamboo. But for Bamboo, communication with a human being is the greatest sin.

SISYPHEAN—DEMPOW TORISHIMA

A strange journey into the far future of genetic engineering, and working life. After centuries of tinkering, many human bodies only have a casual similarity to what we now know, but both work and school continue apace. Will the enigmatic sad sack known only as "the worker" survive the day? Will the young student Hanishibe get his questions about the biological future of humanity answered, or will he have to transfer to the department of theology? Will Umari and her master ever comprehend the secrets of nanodust?

THE THOUSAND YEAR BEACH—TOBI HIROTAKA

Designed in imitation of a harbor town in southern Europe, the Realm of Summer is just one of the zones within the virtual resort known as the Costa del Número. It has been more than a thousand years since human guests stopped coming to the Realm, leaving the AIs alone in their endless summer. But now all that has come to a sudden end, as an army of mysterious Spiders begin reducing the town to nothing. As night falls, the few remaining AIs prepare for their final, hopeless battle… War in the virtual world begins on the shores of *The Thousand Year Beach*.

WWW.HAIKASORU.COM